It Ain't Trickin' If You Got It

3

By: Author First Lady K

This is a work of fiction. Any resemblance to actual events, locales, or persons, living or dead, is entirely coincidental.

Preface

Cindy Black of News 5 stood outside the courthouse ready to report.
"Alright Cindy, you're going live in 3, 2, 1..."

"We're at the Guilford County Courthouse where a shooting has taken place, leaving two people dead. Officers are still trying to piece together information, and are asking anyone that may have any information to please step forward. At this time, the names of the victims have not been released as they await notification to the families. However, from what we gather thus far, allegedly, a woman managed to get her 9 millimeter gun inside of the Guilford County Courthouse past security. Her husband, a defense attorney involved in a current case on the docket, was inside. The alleged shooter came in, opening fire on an open court room, instantly killing one person. The other victim died on the way to the hospital. More details to follow. Stay tuned to News 5 for further updates."

The camera faded, and Cindy removed her earpiece. The media buzzed around the courthouse like a circus. The police commissioner stepped out to give a statement regarding the events.

"What happened today was truly devastating, especially in such a small town as Greensboro. We do have the suspect in custody, and she is being held without bond. While we cannot give information at this time, we have confirmed that two individuals have died, and at least two others are severely injured. We are attempting to locate the families to notify them now, and as we get further information, we will keep you updated. That is all that we have it this time," the commissioner said.

"Commissioner, can you give us the name of the victim that is rumored to have been transported to the hospital and in surgery?" one of the reporters inquired.

"Ah, yes. At this time, that victim has been air lifted to Duke Medical Center. Her parents have been notified and she is in surgery," he responded.

"Can you release the victim's name?" the reporter requested.

"Ah yes, the victim is a recent graduate of North Carolina A&T State University, a member of a well-known African American sorority, she was an honor student by the name of..."

*

Chapter One

"Ok now explain to me what happened." the detective asked Alexis.

Alexis hesitated as she looked over to see her father sitting in disappointment. She never thought it would happen the way it did.

"Answer him. " Her father told her harshly.

He had been crying and she knew he was disappointed with her but wasn't going to say so in front of everyone.

"Everything happened so fast." Alexis told the detective. "I was sitting in the courtroom when the trial was about to begin. I saw Malik coming in but it didn't register that he was Jayshawn's lawyer."

"So this was a coincidence?" the detective inquired. "So you didn't plan this?"

"No!" Alexis snapped. "Why would I do something like this? Don't get me wrong, I mean I'm not gonna lie, I'm glad that he's dead, but I didn't set this up!"

The detective sat looking at Alexis with a stone face. "Now explain to me again how you know the attorney." He asked.

Alexis let out a deep side knowing that she was going to have to explain this for the millionth time. "Like I said before to the judge, before the trial like even started, I let the judge know that I couldn't testify because of the fact that I knew the fucking attorney personally. He and I had been involved in a relationship." She answered starting to get upset.

She could feel the tears stinging eyes from the embarrassment. She could see her father looking at her with anguish.

"Ok and were you aware that he was married?" The detective asked.

"Yes I was." Alexis answered slowly. "He told me about it when I first met him, but I didn't think it would get to this point. I swear!" She stated.

"And to my understanding, he was supporting you financially?" the detective continued.

Alexis looked to see her father's head sit up at the question asked. Her face flushed red.

"Well?" She heard Henderson asked. She was so upset and concentrating on trying to keep her father from being upset, that she forgot he was in the room too.

"Please", she begged in a low tone. "Don't do this."

The detective has a look of irritation on his face. "Ms. Thomas, two people are dead and one severely injured because of your involvement with this man. The fact that you were already in the courtroom because of another man attacking you and he's now dead is more than coincidental." the detective told her angrily. "So Ms. Thomas, please don't think that I'm doing this for sheer amusement. But the fact of the matter is, you are involved in a hell of a lot of problems. So I'm going to ask you again, was the attorney supporting you financially?"

Alexi's eyes grew red with anger. "Yes." she answered through gritted teeth. "Yes he was supporting me financially."

She could see her father drop his head out the corner of her eyes. Henderson got up and walked out of the room slamming the door behind him.

"Baby wait," Alexis tried to stop him. She stood to chase after him but her father stopped her.

"No you're going to sit your ass down and answer these questions." He told her. "Right now that's the last thing you need to be worried about. It's that shit right there that got you in the situation that you're in now." He snapped. "I already told you before that I did not want you with him again because this is all his fault." her father yelled.

"Daddy you're just saying that because of the fact that that you're mad at what's going on right now. It's not his fault. It's all mine." Alexis confessed crying.

The detective sat quiet giving the two a moment to get themselves together before clearing his throat. "Look folks I'm not trying to get in your family business," he told them. "But the fact of the matter is we now have an investigation regarding your daughter." He reminded them looking at her father. "Mr. Thomas I would suggest that you get your daughter an attorney. While your daughter may claim that it looks as if it were coincidental, the fact that Mr. Cheston is dead and he happened to be on trial for the murder of one of her friends is a little bit more than coincidental."

"Wait a minute!" Alexis exclaimed. "So y'all are trying to pin this on me? I know you don't think that I set Jayshawn up to be killed? Yes he killed my friend Tamika. Yes I said I wanted him dead, but I didn't do this. If I did, why would my best friend be dead!" She choked out as she began to cry no longer able to hold in the tears of frustration and hurt.

Listening to how everything sound as she said it out loud she worried because it did sound to be a set up but she couldn't just give up, anger taking over.

"My best friend is gone because that bitch couldn't face me like a woman. Did she tell you how she came to my hotel room and attacked me?" She spat. "No! Did she tell you that she jumped me before I even knew what was going on and beat me to where I ended up in the hospital? Doubtful. So instead of coming after me, you need to be going after her and her fucking husband because they are the ones that are responsible for my best friend being dead! He's the one that lied. He's the one that told me that he was getting a divorce, and I believed him like a dummy."

Her father grabbed her to sit her down as she was now inches away from the detectives face. She saw the detective pull a notepad out of his pocket and write a few pieces of information down.

"Ms. Thomas, were you aware that his wife had hired a private investigator?" He questioned.

Alexis screamed in frustration. "What part of I didn't know that he was still with her don't you seem to understand? No I didn't know she had a private investigator. He told me that they were separated. I can't take this!" She grabbed her purse and stormed out of the room before the detective had a chance to stop her.

Her father ran after her. “Alexis.” he bellowed grabbing her. “Oh so what now you wanna run because shit got real? You mad? You can't get mad at him. He's doing his damn job. I don't even know what to say to you right now.” He said. “I can't believe that you would do something so stupid and just downright dangerous. You really hurt me you know that? You're smart. I know you're smart. I’ve seen your damn grades. I raised you. That means you're too smart to be doing something this stupid!” He fussed. “All over some nigga? What were you thinking? What in your mind said that this was okay? You get any and everything you want. You don’t pay any bills, and I don’t ask you to because I wanted you to focus on school. So I know it isn’t a matter of money because you have not shelled out a dime for anything except your phone bill. So what would make you do that? Huh?” He asked.

“I don't know.” Alexis cried. “I'm sorry. It was just easy.” She said. “I was trying to get over everything that happened with me in Henderson, and I—I--- I don't know. I got caught up in it. It wasn't like I intentionally went to go sleep with a married man.” She assured him.

She cried harder and for the first time her father didn't comfort her.

“You know at some point Alexis,” he told her slowly. “You're going to have to grow up. I'm sorry that you're hurting right now, but look at everything that's happened. I told you so many times before, that everything you do has a consequence. You can't go and do something wrong and not expect to pay the price for it. I know you didn't mean for this to happen baby girl, but it did. And now because of that, two people are dead. Now granted, one of them did not have the best intentions at heart and was a cold-hearted criminal, but at the end of the day he deserved justice here on the earth. And he was not given justice but his life was simply taken from him. And the other was your friend. She did nothing wrong and now; she is gone because she was simply in the wrong place at the wrong time. On top of that, a family, a marriage has been destroyed. This woman’s life was turned upside down. Now this woman is distraught because her family is broken apart and she's going to spend the rest of her life in prison because of what she did to fight for her family. You can't fault her for that. This was a married man with children.” he reminded her. “Did you think how we could affect them? Your best friend is gone Alexis and she's not coming back.” He told her. “I'm not trying to make you feel guilty at all, but you're going to have to own up to some of this. You got a lot of growing up to do.”

There was a moment of silence before he spoke again. "Maybe it's just best if you get out of North Carolina as quickly as possible. I know you're not supposed to start school until the fall, but maybe going down to your grandmothers for a while would do you some good. We'll go to your grandmother's house and you can just get away from everything; because right now, it's no good for you to be here, nor is it safe. I mean every time I turn around somebody is dying." He told her. "Do you know how scared I was when I didn't see you get up? I thought that you were gone." He said choking back tears.

Alexis ran into his arms holding him tightly. "Daddy I'm so sorry." She apologized. "I didn't mean for any of this to happen. I'm so sorry. Please forgive me." She pleaded. "I need you right now." She told him.

He embraced her in a hug and held her tight. "I know baby girl. You just need to make better choices. You know no matter what you do I'm always going to love you. But you gotta start using your head. I'm not trying to bury my daughter."

Alexis sobbed in her father's arms and wished she was anywhere else in the world but the police station. She broke from her father's grasp. "I'm going to step outside and get some air. I'll be back." She promised.

"Okay." Her father answered. "I'll go tell the detective."

Alexis walked outside and saw Henderson's car was still in the parking lot. As she got closer she saw he was sitting in his car. *Might as well deal with this now*, she thought. She went over and tapped on the window.

"Are you going to let me explain?" She asked.

Henderson not looking at her spoke. "What's there to explain? You pretty much just told me everything I needed to know."

"But you don't know that's the thing!" she exclaimed. "I promise you it's nothing like that. It's not like I was out there sleeping around!"

"Oh it's not?" He asked? "Well hell, ever since I met your ass, it's been nothing but dudes. And it's always some type of drama associated with them." He looked at her with anger in his eyes. "If it wasn't my teammate and you trying to fuck him to get back at me, then it's ole boy you dated. And not to speak bad on that nigga cause he dead and all, but the only reason you was with him was because I moved away." He remarked. "Then all this bullshit with Jay Shawn,"

"Now wait a minute!" Alexis interjected. "I did not date Jayshawn, nor did I willingly sleep with him!" Alexis said. "So don't put that on me."

"I'm not saying that you did anything willingly with him, but the point I'm making is that it's more drama. You building up a body count Lex. And now it's some married dude!" He said. "And look at this shit that's behind today, more drama! You fucking with a dude whose wife fucking goes crazy and tries to kill everybody!" He yelled. "What kind of shit is this?"

Alexis could do nothing but stand there and cry. She knew he was right. "But you act like I'm asking for this!" She cried. "I just wanted to be with you." She said.

"Save it Lex. I really don't wanna hear it. You say you wanna be with me but that's not what I'm seeing. And I'm not about to be looking like somebody bitch down here running back to you every time you get done with another nigga. Now if you'll excuse me, I got shit to do. I gotta go explain to my daughter what happened." He told her frustrated.

"Just please try to listen." Alexis pleaded.

Henderson got back in his car ignoring her.

"Don't walk away like this." She begged him. "You're just angry right now."

"Look," Henderson interrupted her. "Being around you is nothing but bad luck. Since the day I met you, you got people coming at you, and now you got a whole new pile of problems. Your life is like a fucking soap opera! Shit! But I'm not about to take a role in it, so it's better that we just part ways now."

Alexis stood stunned at what she was hearing. "I'm sorry." was all she could say.

Henderson took a moment then with his head turning away from Alexis, drove away. Alexis took in everything that Henderson told her. *Am I really that cursed?* She thought to herself. *I can't believe it.* She thought. *After all this and now he's walking away?* She thought. Not knowing what to do, she went back inside to look for her father. *Maybe he was right. Maybe I'll get away from North Carolina all together. The sooner I get out of here the better*. She frowned. *Just start over*. She looked back over her shoulder. "Clearly there's nothing for me here." She said out loud as she continued to look around. She walked back into the police station anxious to start her new life in Atlanta.

*

Chapter Two

Alexis pulled up to her grandmother's house, ready to take her to church. She had been settled in Atlanta for almost six months and was enjoying every minute of it. She had started school a few months ago and was working on her Masters in counseling. She had gone back to North Carolina a few times too speak with the detectives regarding the case, and to testify in court as requested, but after a thorough investigation, the police department had cleared her as a suspect. Marcus' wife had been charged with the murders of JayShawn and Summer, and Alexis could finally move on. Everything was over. She often thought of the good times with her, Summer and Tamika, but she was working through them. She tried to contact Henderson a few times but he changed his number and blocked her on Facebook. She wrote him a letter and sent it to him letting him know everything as to how she felt and pouring her heart out but she never got a response.

She parked her car in her grandmother's driveway and got out. The minute that she got to Atlanta her grandmother told her that she was going to be going to church with her every Sunday. Alexis was extremely reluctant at first, because she wasn't ready to hear someone telling her what she was doing wrong in her life, but after the first couple of services, she found herself liking it. Her grandmother belonged to a Baptist church, and although Alexis was used to the traditional preachers teaching the sermons in ways she couldn't understand, this bishop was different. He spoke to the younger generation in a way that they could understand. She grew to love to attend because she felt as if it was helping her to get on the better path and in her counseling sessions with the bishop, she was able to acknowledge areas she needed to change and where she went wrong.

She used her key to open her grandmother's door. "Nana I'm here! You ready to go?" She yelled walking down the hall. Her grandmother was strict when it came to being on time. If she told her she wanted to be a church by 10:30, than that really meant she wanted to be a church by 10. So Alexis didn't take any chances getting to her grandmother's late.

"Nana!" She called out again. She walked towards her grandmother's bedroom to see that she was still in the bed. "Nana what's going on? What are you still doing in the bed? Now you know we got to be in church in 30 minutes." She reminded her grandmother.

"Baby grandma not feeling good today." Her grandmother told her.

"What's wrong?" Alexis asked.

"Nothing bad baby. I think I got a little bit of that bug that's been going around." her grandmother told her. "But don't worry baby I'll be okay in a few days." She said.

"Okay well I'll go ahead and stay here, that way you can relax and not have to move around as much." She suggested.

"No you going to take your butt to the church." Her grandmother fussed. "Just because I'm sick doesn't mean that you not supposed to go to church. You know what I say about being in the house of the Lord on Sunday." Her grandmother preached.

"Yes ma'am." Alexis laughed. "If you can be out all night Saturday night you should be in the house of the Lord on Sunday morning no matter what." She said mimicking her grandmother.

"Good." Her grandmother told her. "Now you go ahead and go to church, and when you get out of church I'll have dinner ready. Nana gonna make some chicken, greens, mac and cheese, and some pecan pie."

Alexis' stomach began growling just thinking about it. "Now Nana you don't need to be cooking if you're sick." Alexis stressed to her.

"Baby I'm fine. I just need a little bit of rest and then I'll be right back to my old self." her grandmother promised.

"Nana," Alexis said.

"Nana, nothing! Now you get your butt on to that church and make sure you pay attention cause you know I'm going to ask you about the service." Her grandmother warned her.

"Yes ma'am." Alexis promised. "Just promise me that you'll make sure that if you need anything you'll call." Alexis asked her.

"You know I will." Her grandmother said. "You just make sure that you pay attention in that service young lady. And tell your daddy that when y'all finish he needs to come cut this grass."

Alexis laughed. Only her grandmother could be sick and still giving orders from the bed.

"Yes ma'am." She reassured her.

Alexis left her grandmothers and called her father on his cell phone on the way to the church. After several rings, his phone went to voicemail. "Hey daddy. I just left grandma's house and she's not feeling well. She said that she's going to miss church today but that she wants for you to come by and cut the grass. I'm on my way to church now. I'll try to look for you in the lobby." She told him. "I love you. See you in a few."

She hung up her phone and cut her music on as she drove to the church. She thought about where she was 6 months ago and how she was glad that being in Atlanta gave her opportunity to start over. She had been settled in her apartment for the last few months after spending three months at her grandmothers. She was enrolled at Clark Atlanta University and loving her classes. "New life and new opportunities." she said out loud. She commonly said that to herself as reassurance. She was proud of herself because she was focusing on her. *As if I had much of a choice*, she thought.

The minute that she hit Atlanta, her grandmother took over. She made sure that she was up under her every minute of the day. If she didn't have her running errands, then she had her taking her to church, to the grocery store, or introducing her to new friends that she had met since she had gone away to school. And her father was definitely having fun as well. Alexis started to wonder if everything was ok with him and his wife because he spent so much time in Atlanta. She hardly ever saw him call home. She figured she would ask him later when she saw him at church. She was close to pulling into the parking lot when her phone buzzed from an incoming text message. She looked down to see her father had messaged her so she hit the play button for her phone to read back his text.

"Can't make church today. Had to fly home due to an emergency. Everything is fine. Will call you when I land."

Alexis responded to his message.

Alexis: Okay. Have a safe flight.

"Well," she said out loud. "For the first time since I've been here it looks like I'm going to be at the church by myself." She pulled her car into the parking lot. She rushed inside the sanctuary but was stopped at the door by one of the elders.

"Well good morning sister Thomas!" he greeted her.

Alexis pushed a smile. "Good morning." She said as she took the program for the service and prepared to walk past him.

"Now I do not see your grandmother nor your father today!" He told her. "I hope everything is okay?" he questioned.

Alexis was trying to contain her agitation. Her feet hurt in the heels that she was wearing and all she wanted to do was sit down. “Yeah they're fine.” She reassured him. “My dad had a work emergency so he had to fly back home for a few days and Nana is at home with a stomach bug so I told her as soon as I left the church that I would come check on her.” Alexis informed him.

“Well I hate to hear that your grandmother is not feeling well.” He told her. “But it's good to know that she has a wonderful granddaughter to take care of her.”

She gave him a smile and walked inside of the congregation. She was tempted to sit at the back but she could hear her grandmother's voice in her head telling her “The Lord wants you front and center.” She walked further up the aisle towards the pews in the middle of the room. She was dressed in a pencil skirt that went to her knees and ruffled white blouse and was catching attention from most of the male members. She shook her head to herself as she sat down. This don't make no damn sense. And y'all wonder why people don't want to come to church. She thought.

She pulled out her Bible and prepared to enjoy the service. She noticed the Bishop get up and caught his eye as he prepared to give his sermon. He gave her a quick smile and nod before turning his attention to the entire congregation. Alexis flushed red from his glance and felt herself attracted to him. She had not thought about so much as speaking to another man since she came to Atlanta after all that she had been through. She wasn’t sure why she was having the thoughts she was having towards the Bishop, but she knew that she had to fight them off. She was thinking about it so hard, that she missed most of the sermon and was brought back to reality when she heard the organ playing and the Bishop began to do alter call. The service had ended and aside from praise and worship, Alexis hadn’t recalled a thing.

Alexis was on the way to her car leaving the main congregation hall while digging in her purse for her keys when she bumped into one of the Bishops children.

“Oh God, I’m sorry!” she apologized.

“Nah that was my bad shawty.” He told her.

“No, it’s mine.” She laughed. “I wasn't paying attention when I should have been. I was looking for my keys.” She told him.

The boy looked her up and down in what she assumed was admiration. “Aye, you new here?” He asked her.

“Yeah sort of.” She smiled. “My grandmother has been coming to church here for years. I just recently started attending.” She told him.

“Oh okay that’s what’s up.” He told her smiling lightly.

“You're the preacher's son right?” Alexis asked trying to break the ice. It was obvious he was flirting. She saw him smirk.

"Yeah." He answered. "The name is Quinton but everybody calls me Q." He told her introducing himself.

"Oh ok." She told him. "Nice to meet you Quinton." She emphasized teasing him. She saw a smile form across his face.

"So you gonna tell me your name?" He asked.

"Oh! Yea." She laughed not really moving. "My name is Alexis." She said. "My grandmother is Beatrice but everybody calls her Beece cause she says Beatrice makes her sound old."

"Oh word that's your grandma?" He asked her excited. "Man she makes the best peach cobbler." He bragged.

Alexis giggled for a few. "Yes she does. I gotta try to get her to make one soon." She agreed.

The two laughed and Alexis tried to avoid the attraction that she was feeling to him. What the hell is wrong with me? She thought. "Well, she said. Let me go ahead and go. Got to go check on my Nana. She's sick today." She quickly informed him.

"Aight shawty." Quinton said to her. "See you around." He winked at her and walked away.

*

Alexis walked to her car pulling out her cell phone turning it on so that she could check her messages and voicemails. She saw that her father had sent her a message letting her know that he was back in Dallas. She called him before she pulled out of the lot.

"Hey everything okay?" She asked.

"Yeah everything is fine." he answered. "I just had to come back for a few days because there were a few things wrong at the office. But I should be back before you get ready to start fall break next week. I'm aiming to be back by Wednesday." He told her.

"Oh ok." She said. "Well Nana isn't feeling good so I'm going to go check on her and spend the day with her.

"Really?" He asked her. "Did she say what was wrong?"

"Yeah she says she thinks it's just a stomach bug." Alexis told him. "I went over there to pick her up for church and she was still in the bed coughing and wheezing. Soooo, she says that she thinks it's just a stomach bug then I guess she should be fully recovered in a few days."

Her father grunted on the other end of the phone. "Yeah but coughing and wheezing doesn't sound like a stomach bug. That sounds like a cold or the flu or something. You make sure to keep your eye on her." He instructed her.

"Yes father." Alexis stressed. The two talked for a few more minutes before she hung up the phone. Realizing that she still had a voicemail, she checked it.

"This is Detective Williams with the Greensboro Police Department. Alexis, I need you to contact me as soon as possible. There's been new evidence in the case and we need to ask a couple of question. Please return my call at your earliest convenience. The phone number is (336) 420-9720. I look forward to speaking with you. This matter is urgent."

Alexis frowned when she heard the message. Why in the world is Detective Williams calling? She thought. She has been cleared for the case and was no longer a suspect. He wasn't even a part of the case. She met the detective when Collin was killed and her apartment had been broken into. Not sure what to think, Alexis called him. After several rings his phone went to voicemail.

"Hello Detective Williams, this is Alexis Thomas. I was returning your call, when you get opportunity please give me a call back regarding this information. Uh--- I must admit I am a little worried as to what the subject matter pertains to, so, please just call me when you can." She hung up the phone and told herself not to worry about it. She couldn't help but to think about it on the way to her grandmother's house.

Alexis was happy with the way things were going in her life, and had finally started living without looking over her shoulder. She arrived at her grandmother's house and went inside to check on her. She peeked into her grandmother's room to find that she was asleep. Figuring that she would help her grandmother out, she went into the kitchen to begin to work on dinner. Her Nana was known for her cooking, and everybody in the neighborhood would come and get a plate after church on Sunday, so Alexis wanted to make sure that her grandmother didn't have to lift a finger. She knew her grandmother would appreciate it, so she prepared fried chicken, macaroni and cheese, greens, and her favorite, peach cobbler. She was in the middle of cooking when she heard her cell phone ring. Looking on the counter she saw the detective was calling back. She rushed to answer.

"Hello?" she answered.

"Miss Thomas?" He asked.

"Yes this is she. Good afternoon Detective Williams." she answered. "Long time no hear."

"Miss Thomas, I'm sorry to have to interrupt you this Sunday, however there is new news that has been brought to us regarding your ex-boyfriend." He told her.

"Collin?" She asked. "What are you talking about?"

"Well," she heard him sigh. "We have reason to believe that Jayshawn was not involved with his murder."

Alexis was confused and felt knots forming in the pit of her stomach. "What do you mean? I—I--I don't understand."

"From what we have learned," the detective explained. "Colin was killed from blunt force trauma." He explained. "Ballistics found a partial print and it shows that Jayshawn could not have been the one to have killed Colin. The murder that we're looking for is left handed as well. Jayshawn is right handed."

"Okay…" Alexis said "So is it possible that maybe he was using his other hand or something? Like you're saying that he didn't kill my boyfriend now?" Alexis asked angrily. She couldn't believe that she still had to keep reliving what appeared to be this never ending nightmare.

"No. I'm sorry Alexis. Jayshawn couldn't have killed Collin." The detective said frustrated.

Alexis sat down stunned and then it hit her. "Then that means," she responded

"That there are two killers." The detective finish her sentence. "Miss Thomas I don't mean to startle you, nor do I want to scare you, but there are two killers that are involved and although one is dead, there's one that is still out there and you're still potentially in danger." He warned her.

"I just don't understand." She whispered. "Who would want to kill Collin? He did nothing wrong."

"Do you know of anyone that may have wanted to hurt him?" The detective asked.

"No!" Alexis exclaimed. "Collin didn't do anything to anybody. All he did was love me." She began to cry.

"Do you recall anything different about his behavior the last few days you saw him or anybody different hanging around him or anything out of the ordinary with Collin before he died?" The detective inquired.

Alexis thought about it for a few seconds. "No." she said. "The last time I saw Collin, was at my apartment and we were arguing. He left, and I called a few times but he never responded. I saw him on campus a few days later walking with a girl, but I didn't pay it any attention." She told the officer. "I mean, I didn't think anything of it. Like, he had lots of sorority sisters that he would run into on the campus." She told the detective.

"So he was in a fraternity?" the detective questioned. "I didn't see that in his file."

"Yea he was an Alpha." Alexis told him. "But what does that have to do with anything?"

"Nothing." Detective Williams stated. "It just means we need to look into his activity with the organization and see was there any problems. Now this woman you said you saw him with, she could have very well been the last one to see him alive. What did she look like? Did she look familiar to you?" he asked.

"I didn't get a good look at her, so I can't really say who she was." She answered. "All I remember was that she looked a little heavy, and she walked funny. Almost like she was waddling. And she had a tattoo on her back but I couldn't see that far to see what it was."

The detective listened to everything Alexis was telling him. “So the last time you saw him alive was on campus?” He asked her.

“Yeah. We were leaving the campus because they had evacuated the area because of some fire alarm or something and the fire department was there.” She recalled thinking about the fire fighter that she met and exchanged numbers with. She thought about giving him a call just to see how he was.

They had went out a few times but then he confessed to having a girlfriend and didn’t want to create any drama. Alexis was pissed initially, but she was glad he told her. They stopped talking but every now and then they would text each other to see how the other was doing.

“Apparently one of the buildings had a fire alarm go off inside or something.” She explained.

“Hmmm.” He said.

“What does hmmm mean?” Alexis asked him worried.

“Well according to his neighbors, he came home alone with a female that night.” The detective told her. “He was seen going into an apartment with a young lady, but no one could recall who she was.”

Alexis was starting to piece together what the detective was telling her. She felt a twinge of jealousy for a moment knowing that he had brought another girl home. “So do you think that she had something to do with it?” She questioned after a few seconds.

“I don't know.” The detective said. “But I'm damn sure going to find out.” He promised. “In the meantime, you need to make sure to stay out of harm’s way.” He said.

"Of course." Alexis promised him. "But it seems like the harder I try to stay away from drama, the more quickly it finds me." She said.

"I know the feeling." He agreed with her. "But you have to keep trying."

Alexis could hear her grandmother moving in the next room. "Okay well not to cut you off, but I'm at my grandmother's house right now and I don't want her worry about me anymore than she already is so, I will have to talk to you about this later." She whispered quickly rushing to get off the phone.

"Ok. Please call me if you hear anything else?" He asked her.

Alexis hung up the phone as her grandmother walked through the door. "Well hey sleepy head!" She said trying to change her mood. How are you?" She asked her grandmother. "You were asleep for a really long time." She said.

"Yeah baby Nana was more tired than I thought. But I do feel a little bit better now." her grandmother responded.

"Well that's good." Alexis smiled at her grandmother. "Well I started cooking dinner for you so you wouldn't have to do much."

"I see." Her grandmother smiled looking at her granddaughter in the kitchen. "What you got cooking in here girl?" She asked laughing.

"Just some chicken and macaroni and cheese and greens." Alexis told her. "I know it ain't like yours but it's close." she joked.

"Honey," her grandmother told her, "It ain't gotta be like mine. Chile from the way it's looking in here it's better than mine."

Alexis laughed.

"Now what was going on just a second ago? You alright?" Her grandmother asked sternly.

Alexis let out a sigh. She knew that she couldn't keep anything from her grandmother. "Nana… I'm trying so hard. For the last four months I haven't really thought about anything that happened when I was in Greensboro. I was starting to get over losing Henderson and Mika and Summer being killed. I was finally starting to move on and then I get a phone call today from Detective William telling me that there's been a new development in the case." She stopped to see her grandmother's concerned expression.

"Baby what new developments?" her grandmother looked nervous.

"Apparently JayShawn didn't kill Collin. The detective called me and said that ballistics showed that there was no way Collin was killed by Jayshawn." Alexis told her grandmother.

"Well then who did?" Her grandmother inquired.

"I don't know." Alexis said. "But I was the last one to see Collin alive apparently and it could have been with the person that killed him when he was on campus the day when then fire alarms went off."

"Well now no need to worry yourself sugar. Do the police have any leads?" She asked her.

"I don't know. But I hope they find out something soon because I'm tired of living my life like this Nana. Like it just seems like it's never ending pattern." Alexis confessed. "I'm trying to do right and live the life I'm supposed to live, but I keep getting sucked back into drama. Like God is punishing me constantly! I know I did wrong in the past, but how much longer should I be punished for it?" She asked aggravated.

"Now you stop that!" her grandmother fussed. "I don't ever want to hear you talking like that. Don't you ever question God. It's not punishment. Never think that. Now HE may be testing you. But never punishing. Like I always tell you, your test will be your testimony. And right now you feel like you have no other option, no other way. But baby whether you realize it or not, God is making a way. But believe me when I say this baby, it will get better. Unfortunately you made some decisions in the past that are coming back to bite you in the ass."

Alexis' eyes grew large. It was rare that her grandmother ever cursed so when she heard it she was a little surprised.

"I know Nana and that's what I'm trying to fix." Alexis said frustrated. "I think somethings wrong with me." She confessed in a whisper.

Her grandmother laughed hearty laugh before she began coughing. "Now what in the world is wrong with you? You're young, beautiful, educated, you got a lot going for you girl. So what could possibly be wrong with you?"

Alexis sighed. "I don't know if I should say it." She whispered lowering her head from embarrassment.

"Child please." Her grandmother scoffed. "You can't tell me nothing that I never heard before."

Alexis thought about the feelings that she had in church with the pastor and the attraction she had to him. She swallowed hard before speaking. "Nana I think I have a problem." She said to her slowly. "I think I may be...addicted to…"

"Addicted to what baby?" Her grandmother asked.

"Men." Alexis answered bluntly.

Her grandmother got quiet and Alexis saw a smile form on her face. “Well honey I must be too. Because if it wasn't for men, shoot you wouldn't be here now.” She choked laughing.

Alexis stared at her grandmother and tried to keep a straight face. “Oookay.” She said while laughing. “But seriously Nana, all I think about is different guys. I met a guy today at church and I was trying not to flirt with him but I couldn't help myself.” She admitted.

“Baby its natural.” Her grandmother giggled. “You're going to see guys and you are going to be attracted to them. It's just a part of life. The trick is to control your urges. And hopefully you're not getting too many of those urges. But it will be good for you to date a church boy.”

What about a church man? Alexis thought to herself. She did not tell her grandmother that she had a physical attraction to the pastor because she knew she would never hear the end of it. “So you think that this is okay?” Alexis asked her.

“Yes sugar. You’re young.” Her grandmother reassured her. You’re gonna make stupid mistakes. I would much rather that you come to me or your father and at least talk to us rather than go out there and just do something stupid. Trust me your daddy used to do a lot of dumb stuff. But he got it together.” Her grandmother grabbed her by the hand. “Alexis you gotta live your life. You messed dup, lesson learned. Now you know that you got to make wise decisions. Not everything will be easy, don't get me wrong. But you can't scrutinize everything that you do. You're going to make mistakes. So just relax baby.” Her grandmother told her.

Alexis smiled at her grandmother hugging her.

"Thanks Nana. I'm glad I could talk to you because daddy would have shipped me to a convent or something." She joked. "Now back to you!" She changed the subject. "Daddy said that I better take care of you and that you better sit your butt down somewhere." She joked with her.

"Your daddy better hush up before I take a belt to his tail!" her grandmother responded. "I told you it was nothing but a stomach bug I don't know why you went and told him anyway." She said.

Alexis became serious. "Because that is my job as your grandbaby. You were like my mommy when my own mom gave me up so I gotta go tell daddy. And a stomach bug don't have you coughing like that." She corrected her. "I just want to make sure that you're good. So tomorrow I'm going to take you to the doctor."

"The hell you are, I am fine!" Her grandmother said. "That's right I said it."

Alexis could not help but laugh at her grandmother's stubbornness. "Like I said, tomorrow young lady we're going to go to the doctor and then you going to make me a peach cobbler!" She laughed.

"Girl take your butt over there and go wash them greens fore I go cut a switch." She grumbled.

Alexis jumped off the bar stool that she was sitting on and went to do what her grandmother asked her to. She would worry about all the other stuff later.

*

Ariane sat in her apartment with the television on halfway paying attention. She had been keeping a low profile ever since the trial. She remembered the woman screaming in the courtroom and bullets flying. She also remembered the look on JayShawn's face when he saw her sitting behind Alexis. As angry as she was at him for the things she still loved him with all her heart and wanted to cry out when that woman took his life. She had to contain her tears for fear that someone in the courtroom would realize the connection with him.

Thinking about it outraged her, and all she could wonder was how happy Alexis probably was now that he was dead. Ariane had tried to move on herself, but everyone that she dated she compared to JayShawn. She couldn't seem to stay away from the bad boys, but none of them were like the love of her life.

If I hadn't pressed charges, that bitch would be dead now, she thought to herself. She constantly blamed herself for JayShawn being arrested. *Keisha was just some bird. Hell, I could have took care of her.*

Reminiscing, she was near tears and was feeling depressed until she saw JayShawn's face on the television screen. She quickly reached for her remote to turn the television up as she saw the words "SEARCHING FOR ACCOMPLICE" flashed across the screen.

"This is April Spry with News 5. Investigators have given an update on the murder of Collin Strong Jr. the North Carolina A&T student that died about 6 months ago and the connection to JayShawn Cheston. Recall that Cheston was arrested and charged a few years ago for the rape and attempted murder of Alexis Thomas. During his time in prison, Cheston cleverly managed to escape and shortly after that escape, a spree of murders occurred. Tamika Cheston, sister to Jayshawn as well as Collin Strong Jr. were murdered supposedly at the hands of the now deceased Cheston. Cheston was killed in a courtroom shoot out you may remember from a few months prior. Police have now given an update saying that Cheston was not responsible for Strong's murder, and that there is a second accomplice. Strong was last seen with an African American woman between 18 to 25 years old, on the campus of North Carolina A&T State University. Police say she is not a suspect at this time, however is wanted for questioning. Police are asking residents if you have any leads or know the woman last seen with Strong, please contact the tip line at (336) 555-1000."

Ariane froze and her heart began to race. *How the fuck did they figure that shit out?* She thought to herself. *I made sure that there weren't any witnesses.* Ariane started to panic and rushed to her phone. She called her brother for his help.

"What's up baby sis?" he answered.

"Hey I need your help with something." She rushed.

"Alright what is it? A car? Some clothes? What you need money for now?" He asked.

"I can't really get into much of it over the phone, but I need to go out of town for a while. I need to hold about 5,000 dollars to get me settled." She explained.

"$5,000?" He asked her seeming upset. "What kind of trouble are you in that you need "5,000?"

"Like I said, I can't really get into it over the phone, but I'll get it back to you with interest." She promised.

"Where you trying to go?" He asked her.

"Anywhere. I just got to clear my head."

"Alright I got you." He said. "I may be able to help you out with a place to stay. I got a couple of spots in Georgia". Her brother told her.

"Oh word?" She asked.

"Yeah. I bought a house out in Atlanta about four years ago and rented it to college students. It's a guaranteed way for me to make money. Especially in a city like Atlanta where it's all of those college students." He informed her.

Ariane thought about his offer and remembered that Alexis was in Atlanta going to school. "You know what? That is perfect." She said with a smile on her face. "ATL here I come." She grinned.

"Alright meet you at your house tomorrow morning with all of the details." He told her.

"Cool." Arian agreed. "I'll see you in the morning bro. I appreciate it." She thanked him.

"No prob sis." He said

Ariane ended her call and a sinister laugh escaped. "This is too fucking perfect." She said to no one. "I'll make sure that Alexis never has the opportunity to go to the police." she said. She was almost giddy with excitement of being in Atlanta and making sure Alexis couldn't connect the dots.

*

Chapter Three

"Beatrice I'm going to be honest with you. This is not looking good." Alexis was sitting in the doctor's office with her grandmother. She had scheduled the appointment for her when she saw that her cough was getting worse. Alexis appeared frightful and hoped that nothing bad would happen.

"Well, doctor, what is it? I mean, she said that she just had a bug. I didn't think that a bug would make her cough like that so, what is it?" Alexis asked him nervous.

The doctor looked from Alexis to her grandmother confused. "You haven't told her?" he questioned.

Alexis looked at the doctor as if he was crazy. "Told me what?" she barked. She noticed her grandmother had become suddenly nervous. "Nana what is he talking about? What's going on? What haven't you told me?" she rattled off.

Tears were forming in her grandmothers eyes. "Baby," she announced. "I've been sick for a while now. I didn't want to tell you because I know how much you worry."

"Okay but you're getting better though right? Alexis inquired. "Like is it just something that you need to take medicine for or what?"

"No baby. Unfortunately it's not something that I can just get better at." Her grandmother answered shaky.

"I don't, I don't understand. What's going on? What are you not telling me?" Alexis asked as she looked back and forth between her grandmother and the doctor.

Her grandmother shed a tear and the words that Alexis heard come out of her mouth almost stopped her heart from beating. "Baby I've got stage 4 lung cancer." She admitted.

Alexis went numb to the news her grandmother gave her. "What?" She whispered. "Lung cancer? No! No that can't be right! It just can't be."

"Yes baby." Her grandmother sniffled. "I'm sorry."

"Nana NO!" Alexis yelled. "It's not right. It can't be right! It just, it- it- it can't." she cried before completely breaking down.

Her grandmother grabbed her in a hug. "Baby it's going to be ok. I have led a strong and wonderful life. I'm at peace with this."

"But it's not fair." Alexis wept. "Why didn't you say something?" She asked her.

"Well Lexi like I said," her grandmother responded. "With everything that was going on with you, I wasn't about to add stress to that. Plus even if I did tell you what would that change?" She asked. "Like I said baby it's my time. I'm okay with it."

"But I'm not!" Alexis screamed. "I don't understand how you can sit here and be so calm about this. You're dying! But you want to sit here and act like everything is okay she bawled."

"Because it is Alexis." Her grandmother objected. "Despite what you think, it's okay. It's a part of life. Whether you want to accept it or not, death is a part of life. We all are put on the earth to die at some point. It's not like I'm dying young baby. If you only knew half of the life that I've lived. I'm okay with leaving this earth. I don't want to be on this earth forever." She proclaimed.

Alexis sniffled and try to contain her cries. "How long have you been sick?" She asked her seriously.

"I've known now for close to a year."

"A year!" Alexis jumped up. "You mean to tell me you've known for a year that you had lung cancer and you didn't say ANYTHING to me? Does daddy know?" She ranted.

Her grandmother lowered her head and swallowed the lump that was forming in her throat. She knew her granddaughter would be upset but, not she was trying to protect her.

"No he doesn't. And I don't want you saying anything to him either. I want to go my way. I know your daddy is going to want me to take all these different kinds of specialists and see all these doctors, but I'm not going to do that. So you need to promise me that you can keep your mouth shut." Her grandmother begged.

Alexis shook her head back and forth. The doctor sat in the room quiet and allowed the two to talk without interruption.

"I don't understand how you could keep something like that from me Nana. We tell each other everything. You just told me last night that I didn't have to worry about keeping anything from you. But yet you kept something so big for me. And now, you want me to keep it from my father, your son, and not say anything? I can't do that. I'm sorry but I love you too much and care about you too much." She stressed.

Alexis turned her head towards the doctor. "How long does she have? Is this treatable? "

The doctor looked at her grandmother for confirmation that he could share the information. Her grandmother just shook her head up and down in agreement. The doctor now looked at Alexis with genuine concern. “At most she has about a month. For a while she was doing chemo but it was not effective. I would go ahead and start making plans now.”

Hearing the doctor tell her that her grandmother didn't have much time, Alexis broke down and cried harder than ever. The doctor excused himself from the room to give them some time.

“Alexis baby you got to pull yourself together.” Her grandmother fussed. “You really gotta stop. You're going to make yourself sick.”

Alexis felt as if she was losing a sense of reality. She hugged her grandmother tightly and cried hard. “Nana please don't leave me. Please don't leave me.” she pleaded. “I need you.”

Seeing her granddaughter hurting, she began to cry. “I promise you baby, I'm going to be here always. Nana taught you well, so I know you're going to do the right thing in your life. You just gotta apply yourself. Now you gotta stop all that carrying on. You got Nana in here crying.” She laughed to lighten the mood.

Alexis dried her eyes and continued to cry softly. "Yes ma'am." She responded. She knew that her Nana was trying to be strong for her, but she just couldn't think about her life without her Nana. Especially after the last few months of spending so much time with her. She could still hear the words in her head of the doctor telling her that she only had a month to live. Realizing those words only angered her more. *Why does my grandmother have to die?* She thought. *I have lost everybody! Now I got to lose my Nana. Is this the kind of game that you're playing with me God? So you take away my best friend, my boyfriend, and now you want to take away my Nana? But I'm supposed to have faith in You?* She questioned. *I'm supposed to believe in you? How can I believe in somebody that can just take everything from me? What kind of test is this? This is a test? No, this is hell.*

Almost as if she was reading her thoughts she heard her grandmother say, "No matter what you think baby do not lose your faith in God. I know it's hard right now with everything that you've gone through, but God will not disappoint you. He will never forsake you."

"Like hell He will." Alexis mumbled.

Her grandmother frowned at her. "I know this is not my granddaughter talking like that." She snapped. "You know better. I've taught you better. I don't care what you may be feeling right now Alexis Latrice Thomas, but don't you EVER let me catch you talking like that. Now I know you're mad. So am I! But being mad is not going to change things. Being mad is not going to make me better. Turning your back on God, is not going to make this cancer go away. It's not. And I'm not going to tolerate you acting like some heathen right now."

"But Nana!" Alexis interjected.

"But Nana nothing!" her grandmother continued cutting her off. "I don't wanna hear it. Now this is a time where family is supposed to come together. I'm not saying that you can't be upset, but you will not talk like that in front of me. You take that up with Him on your own time." She said pointing up as if pointing to the heavens.

"Yes ma'am." Alexis answered solemnly. She didn't want to upset her grandmother any further but she knew what little faith that she had was now gone. She gathered her bag and helped her grandmother walk out to the car to head home to break the news to her father.

*

The Bishop walked into the hospice to find Miss Beece laying in the bed with her son and granddaughter watching television. *That's where I know her from*, he thought to himself. Miss Beece's granddaughter had attended his church and she caught his attention a few times. She was gorgeous and he had impure thoughts of her at times, why he didn't know, but here she was staring him face to face. Judging by the look on Alexis face, she had some of the same uncomfortable thoughts.

"Well hello there young lady," Bishop said to break the awkward silence.

"Hello Bishop!" Miss Beece said as a smile formed on her face. "I'm so glad you came." She said.

"Of course. You know I have to come and make sure that you are in here behaving yourself. You have to get better lady so that I can see you in the third-row pew Sunday," he said.

They both knew that the likelihood of her being released from the hospital was slim. Miss Beece had told him and the church of her being diagnosed with cancer and had decided against treatment so her days were numbered. She told the doctors that she didn't want to spend her remaining days taking treatments that although were intended to help her body, would cause severe pain.

"If the Lord intends for me to stay on His earth, then He will make a way." She would tell her doctors, family, and friends.

Miss Beece smiled at Bishops words and said "Well Bishop, as much as I would like for that to happen, I think it's time for me to go home. My soul is a little tired."

A hush fell over the room and everyone looked sad at her words. She spoke up quickly. "Bishop I do apologize. I failed to introduce you to my family. This is my son Melvin Thomas. He came here to visit for a while from Tennessee. And this here is my granddaughter, Alexis. Alexis is here in grad school over at Clark Atlanta. You've seen her before at church with me. She's Melvin's daughter." She said proudly.

Bishop shook hands with both of them. "It's nice to meet you. I'm sorry that we had to meet under these circumstances. Mr. Thomas, you should know that your mother is a wonderful part of our church. She was there before I became a pastor and was just a knucklehead running the streets." He said with a light laugh.

Mr. Thomas shook his head and smiled as well.

"Miss Beece here has a way of getting people to listen to her. That's the kind of leadership we needed at the church. She's part of the reason why I became a pastor. I used to be in the streets and she told me to get my life together. Of course, I shrugged it off and was hard headed but, your mother, this wonderful woman, wouldn't give up on me. Now I'm walking Gods path thanks to her." He took her hand and squeezed it.

Miss Beece smiled and wiped a tear. "That's because I knew what God had in store for you son. You've had a rough past and your rough days aren't behind you. Now I don't say much on it but, I know what's going on between you and Quinton. Now I don't know the whole story and it my business to know, but what I do know is, that boy doesn't belong in them streets. Now I know you love your son. You got to save him and show him the way to God."

Bishop not wanting to be disrespectful listened to what she had to say. "Yes ma'am. I am praying for him to come home every day. Now I don't want you to be worrying about that right now Miss Beece. I want you to just relax and take care of yourself."

Miss Beece wasn't stopping. "I'm good and relaxed son so no need to worry about that. You got to do more than pray to save your son. You got to go and get him Bishop. You know coming from them streets what they can do to that boy. Don't let him go down that path. There is still time. I tell my grandbaby here the same thing. Now if you really want me to get better, you go and bring that boy home. That will make me better." She said in a stern voice.

"Yes ma'am." He said. He looked over at Alexis' father, who was giving an apologetic look.

"Now you see what I went through as a kid," her father said with a laugh. "She is not just going to let something go."

"That's my Nana," Alexis said with a smile as she kissed her grandmother on the cheek.

"That's right baby. Now Nana is getting tired. I think I need to rest for a little bit." Miss Beece said.

"Ok, Miss Beece, I'm going to go ahead and let you get your rest. I will come and see you tomorrow okay?" Bishop asked her.

"That's alright son. You just remember what I said." She told him.

Bishop, Alexis and her father walked out the room as Miss Beece settled to go to sleep. When they reached the hallway, her father laughed a little more.

"Sorry about that in there. When my momma gets on something, it's hard to get her to let it go." Her father joked.

Bishop shook his head in laughter. "I understand brother. It's ok. I see her every Sunday in the church fussing at a few members so I know."

"Yea when I came here to go to school, she told me the first day that I needed to find a church home," Alexis joined in.

"Well, I'm glad that you chose Pearly Gates. If you ever need anything, my doors are always open." Bishop told her trying not to make eye contact.

"Thank you, Bishop. I appreciate that. We look forward to seeing you Sunday and please continue to keep my grandmother in your prayers." She asked solemnly.

"Of course." Bishop pulled out his card and handed one to both her and her father. "My number is on that card. Please don't hesitate to call. Good evening." He said as he walked back towards his car.

*

"Father, I come to you as humbly as I know how. Lord, this is hard for me because I feel like I am being a hypocrite coming in your house and asking you for forgiveness when I know that I'm probably going to go out there and do worse. Lord I know that you are tired of me apologizing but my son is a reminder of how far I have come and I don't want to lose him to the very thing that I got caught up in. Father I ask that you please watch over me as well as my family during this very trying time. Especially Tanya, we both know that she is stubborn and doesn't want to step aside easily. Keep her safe so that if something does happen to me, she will be there for our son," the pastor prayed.

The pastor continued to silently pray when he heard the doors of the church open. He turned around to see a woman walking down the aisle towards him. As she got closer, he saw it was Alexis, Ms. Beece's granddaughter.

"Alexis?" he called out to her.

Alexis walked up to him as he got up from the altar. The closer that she got, he could tell that she had been crying.

"I didn't think that I would find you here this early." She told him as he embraced her in a quick hug.

"Yea I normally am not here this early however I had a few things on my heart this morning that I needed to go to God with." He told her as he motioned for her to sit on the pew.

"Sounds like you and me both." She told him as she felt the tears stinging her eyes.

He saw how her face changed and got concerned. "Hey, hey, hey what's wrong? What's going on?" he asked her now worried.

Alexis took a deep breath before she completely broke down in tears. "Nana passed away last night!" she sobbed almost falling out of the pew. Bishop grabbed her and held her to keep her from falling.

"Okay, wait a minute. Slow down." He told her as he tried to understand what she was saying. "Okay, now talk to me. What happened?" he asked.

Alexis collected herself and spoke slowly. "Last night, grandma passed away. Me and daddy went back inside and she asked us to go to the cafeteria to get her something to eat. We went down there and decided to stop at the gift shop to get her some of her favorite flowers. When we got back, she was dead!" she wailed. "Wh-wh-, while we were downstairs, she told the doctor that she was tired of dealing with it and wanted him to unplug her. We asked him why did he let her do it and he said he saw how tired she was and that he couldn't argue with her anymore. Why did she leave me?" she cried out as she crumpled yet again.

Bishop grabbed her and hugged her close. "Alexis I wish I knew what to say right now to ease your heart from this pain." He said as she continued to cry on his shoulder. Bishop did the only thing that he knew how to do; pray. "Lord," he said "Alexis is hurting right now from the loss of her grandmother. Father we know that although she's not here in the physical sense, you called her home for a reason. But we need you to help Alexis heal Lord. Help her and her family get through these tough times. Let your spirit surround her in these times ahead Father." He prayed. Bishop continued to sit at the pew and hold Alexis as she wept.

"Just let it out." He said.

Alexis spoke out as in between sobs. "I just don't want to believe it. She was like a mother to me." She said as she began to slow her cries. "She was the only one in my family that didn't make me feel like crap for the things I've done. She didn't judge me. She didn't make me feel like an outcast." She said sniffling.

Bishop looked concerned with what she was telling him. "Why would you feel like an outcast?" he asked her.

Alexis was about to speak when the door opened and they both turned to see three men enter the Church. As they got closer, Bishop saw that it was the maintenance men that were there to fix the roof.

"Good morning gentlemen." He said as he looked at his watch. "I'm assuming you are here to fix the roof?" he asked.

"Yes sir." One of the men answered.

Bishop stood and motioned for Alexis to follow him. "Well, we will get out of your way." He said as he watched one of the men staring at Alexis. "Alexis do you want to continue this in my office?" he asked her. Alexis shook her head in agreement and followed him to the office.

Bishop walked down the hallway ahead of Alexis and shed a few tears for Miss Beece. He thought about what she had told him on his last visit to the hospital. He got to the door and unlocked it cutting the light on. He stepped to the side so that Alexis could step in.

"Come on in," he said as he placed his keys on the desk. Alexis took a seat on the sofa that was in the corner and Bishop closed the door behind him sitting down at his desk.

"Now you were telling me something about feeling like you were an outcast?" he asked her.

Alexis shook her head. “Yea.” She took a couple of deep breaths and explained. “When I was growing up, I didn’t have my mother around. So my father took care of me with the help of my grandmother. I developed early as a child. My cousins used to always tease me about the way that I looked and I’m not gonna lie, I started messing with boys early. When my cousins found out, they made fun of me and called me a whore and everything that you could think of.” She paused as she felt tears forming again.

Bishop reached over to his desk to retrieve a box of tissues and handed them over to her.

“What they didn’t know is that my mother's husband was abusing me. I was told that the only thing I was good for was lying on my back.” Alexis started to get angry. “I didn’t know how to tell them but my father found out and told my grandmother. She told me that everything was going to be okay and that I didn’t do anything wrong. As I got older, I did whatever I wanted to with whoever I wanted. I really didn’t see anything wrong with what I was doing because I was honest with them you know?” she said. Bishop shook his head listening to everything that she was saying. “I never lied to anybody and I always kept it 100 with them. I just am tired of having to cry all the time. In the past year and half so much has happened. I’ve been kidnapped, raped, my boyfriend was killed, then I lost my both my best friends, I had some married chic after me, and now this! My Nana was all I had.” She told him as she let herself fall apart.

Bishop stood to walk over towards the couch. He sat next to her and grabbed her hand. "Let me tell you something." He said. "Your grandmother is extremely proud of the woman that you are. Now granted, I have not known you your entire life, but I can tell that if Miss Beece had a hand in raising you, that you are an alright person and if you are anything like your grandmother, I know you are a strong woman." He told her with a chuckle to try to cheer her up.

Alexis smiled thinking about how stubborn her grandmother was. Her father always reminded her of how much like her that she was.

"Yea that's true. It just…seems so surreal." Alexis said. "I mean I just found this out! And then when she told us, I just thought she would fight harder." She gripped his hand harder and leaned on his shoulder. "Oh God!" she cried. "Please give her back!"

Bishop rubbed her back with one hand and continued to hold her hand with the other as he attempted to soothe her. He was completely at a loss for words, but he didn't want to leave her alone. He was supposed to meet his boy Deuce to deal with his own issues, but he was still a pastor.

She looked up at him with tears streaming down her face and he felt his manhood starting to rise looking at her. Attempting to ignore his urge, he handed her a tissue to wipe the tears off her face. She looked at him and slowly leaned towards him kissing his lips. Bishop kissed her back, and shortly after, realizing what he was doing, backed away.

"Alexis, this is wrong. You're not really thinking clear." He said to her barely able to resist her.

She placed her fingers over his lips.

"Please." She requested. "Just, let me have this."

Alexis kissed Bishop again while unzipping her jacket. She revealed her breasts to him and began to kiss on his neck while she massaged his growing manhood. He lay her down on the couch on top of her and began to massage her breasts. She pulled her skirt up and Bishop unbuckled his pants. He slid her panties to the side and entered her quickly, pumping in and out of her with such force. Both were soothing each other's hurt. They were giving each other temporary relief for their own bad situations. Bishop began to pump faster as he felt himself about to explode. He gripped her hand tightly as they both exploded together. The two lay there on his couch for a few moments panting heavily trying to catch their breath. Bishop sat up as he looked down at Alexis. Quietly, they both began to fix their clothing and straighten up knowing that what they had just done was wrong.

"I guess I should leave you to your business," Alexis said as she zipped her jacket back up.

Bishop stood and went to sit back in his seat massaging the temples of his head. *What the hell did I just do?* He thought to himself. *I just had sex with this girl in the church*! He thought. His head was spinning at the thought of what he had just done.

"So will you do it?" Alexis asked snapping him out of his thoughts.

"I'm sorry. Do what?" he asked.

"I said that my dad and the rest of the family may need someone there to help them. And of course when the arrangements are being made I know they will want you to give the eulogy." She said.

"Oh, of course." He said. "I will stop by later on this evening and check on the family."

"Thanks." She said as she avoided looking him in the eyes. "Ok well, I have to go. Sorry about…you know." She said as she left the office.

Alexis closed the door and rushed to her car leaving Bishop in the office. Alexis ran to her car, jumping in and locking the doors as if she was being chased. *Oh my god what the hell did I just do?* She thought to herself. *I can't believe that I just had sex with this man in the church!* She had been a ball of emotions, and did not go in there with the plan to sleep with him. She knew that if her grandmother could see her, she would be so disappointed. Although the feeling was good at the time, Alexis felt so guilty. *I can't believe that I slept with the pastor in the church.* She thought.

"I'm fucking crazy!" She yelled out loud. "I can't believe I did that shit."

She began punching the steering wheel crying in frustration and agony. She was so upset and distraught with everything that she was dealing with emotionally. "I'm sick of this shit!" she started screaming.

Sobs escaped her as she continued to scream. "Why? Why do you keep fucking with me? When is it enough? I'm supposed to believe in you before what? All you do is inflict pain. Well no more!" She yelled. "From now on I'm doing things my way. I try to do right, and all I get is wrong. You took my boyfriend from me, you took my best friends from me, you put nothing but crazy people in my damn life, and now you take the one person that gave a shit about me besides my father. What? Are you going to take him next? Is that what you got planned for me? Well I won't sit and wait for it anymore. You hear me? No more!"

She gripped the steering wheel to keep from punching and damaging her car.

Tap! Tap! Tap!

She almost jumped out of her skin when she heard someone knocking on the window. She looked to see Quinton standing looking at her.

"Yo shawty you alright?" He asked. "You not in here like flipping out and shit are you?" He asked her looking nervous. He was getting out of his car when he noticed her spazzing.

"No it's not! It's not fine!" She snapped. "I'm trying so hard to hold it together, but I can't." She strained. "I can't hold it together! I'm trying to hold it together but I just can't okay? Everybody keep saying that it's going to be fine, but it's not! Everybody that I know and love is dying around me! How can I be fine with that? You know the amount of shit that I have gone through these last few years? It's a surprise that I'm not dead by now. Maybe that's what the fuck I need to do is just kill my fucking self! Maybe then people will finally just leave me the hell alone and I will stop being a fucking target! I have lost everything and everyone! I've had to move to get away from muthafuckas trying to kill me!" She raged.

"Ok whoa, whoa, whoa, whoa calm down." Quinton stopped her. "I really need you to calm down right now shawty. Come on get out the car and let's go for a walk." He asked her calmly.

Alexis was gripping the steering wheel so hard that her knuckles were turning white. Loosening her grip, Quinton opened her car door to help her out.

"Right now you really shouldn't be driving." He told her. "So, we'll just go for a walk until you calm down. If you want, I can call somebody and have them come get you."

"I just… I can't deal with this right now." She gritted. She began to cry for what seemed like the millionth time that day.

"Okay so you want to tell me what happened?" He questioned her. He didn't know much about her, but to see her crying, got to him in a way he hadn't felt.

"My grandmother passed away last night." she belted out.

"Miss Beece?" He asked her.

"Yeah!" She wailed.

He let out a deep sigh. "Damn shawty I'm sorry to hear that. She was a real cool lady." He professed. "Are you going to be ok?" He asked her?

"No." She wept harder. "No I'm not going to be okay. I'm so tired of fighting. I'm so tired of having to go through all of this shit! Everybody else can live a happy life but me. I keep having to deal with the dumb shit." She exclaimed.

The two had walked towards Quinton car. Alexis leaned against it to try to stop herself from shaking. "I'm sorry. I'm really not trying to bring any of my drama to you. But you just caught me on a bad day." She sniffed.

Quinton snorted. "Trust me shawty, it ain't bothering me in the least bit. You good. I just didn't want you going red rum and shit in the parking lot. But on the real though, do you need me to call somebody?" He asked her.

Alexis laughed sarcastically. "I mean really who else is there to call? The people that were close to me ain't here no more." She mumbled holding her head down.

"Aight shawty I tell you what," he said "Why don't you roll with me for a little bit. I'll take you around and we'll go grab a bite to eat or something." He suggested.

"Oh no don't go through all that trouble." She dismissed his invitation. ".

"I didn't mean to interrupt you or anything like that. Besides, what are you doing at the church anyway? From what my grandmother told me, you and your pops don't really get along. And no shade, but, you don't really have the best reputation." She responded hesitantly.

"You right." He said throwing his hands up in mock surrender. "I wasn't coming here to the church to see my Pops though. I was coming here to meet my sister to get some information about a dance or something, but I can hit her up and tell her to meet me later. Right now, I really don't think you should be by yourself or trying to drive. I mean, if you want, I could put you on the bus." He laughed.

First time that day, Alexis smiled. "Whatever." She said. "Just try to have me back at my car in a couple hours if you can. I got to start helping with funeral arrangements soon and I don't want my daddy to worry. But I just need to get away for a while and clear my head."

"Aight cool." He agreed. "I'll take you to one of the hot spots to get something to eat. You ever been to Sweet Georgia's Juke Joint?" He asked.

"Boy please." she said "I haven't been able to do anything. And with my Nana, she was the best restaurant in town. I wish I would go try to eat somewhere else knowing that she cooks at the drop of a dime." She held her head down and reminisced on how her grandmother fussed at her for eating junk food.

Quinton noticed how quite she was suddenly. "My bad sorry I didn't mean to bring up the memories."

"Oh no it's okay." Alexis said. "I don't want to forget my grandmother. No need to apologize. You didn't do anything wrong."

Quinton walked over and open the passenger door to his car for Alexis. "Hop in."

Alexis climb inside of Quinton's black on black BMW.

"Ain't nothing in this car that I need to worry about is it? Like something that may get me in jail?" She inquired.

"Nah shawty you good." He got in the driver's side and cranked the car.

The two drove through Peachtree towards the restaurant. "So tell me about yourself." He spoke. "What brought you Atlanta?"

Alexis shrugged. "Well, I had some stuff going on in Greensboro, and my father thought it would be best if I got out of North Carolina for a while." She said. "I applied for Clark Atlanta as well as a few other schools for grad school in the area, and he wanted me close enough to him but still far enough to where I can have my own freedom. So I went ahead and decided on Clark Atlanta. I wasn't supposed to be moving so soon but with everything that happened back home, I had to get away for safety reasons. So I've been here ever since taking care of my Nana and going to school."

Quinton drove silently listening to Alexis. "That's what's up." He said. "What are you studying?"

Alexis smirked. "Believe it or not counseling". She said.

Quentin grunted a laugh. "Well they say the best way to teach others to get over something is to experience it yourself." He told her light hearted.

"I guess." She mumbled. "I haven't really had a chance to do much here because I've been with my Nana most of the time, but every now and then I may go out and get to see the city a little bit." She told him.

"Aye well whenever you want to see the city shawty just give me a holler and I'll come scoop you. You know since you in my town." He grinned.

Is this nigga trying to flirt right now? She asked herself. "Ok." She agreed dismissing his gesture.

The two pulled up to the restaurant and Quinton got out of the car to open Alexis door. "Now I'm letting you know, this food might give your Nana's a run for her money."

Alexis grew quiet for a moment. Trying not to cry, she forced a smile on her face and followed Quinton into the restaurant.

"So what's up with you?" She sought to change the subject. "How is it that a preacher's kid has such a bad reputation?"

"Oh my story is easy shawty." He told her as they sat down in the booth of Sweet Georgia's Juke Joint. "My Pops used to be a major drug dealer back in the day. Everybody still talks about the living legend bishop." He explained. "But now, he's been a pastor for the past almost 15 years. My mom used to mess around while he was with the 'first lady'," he said rolling his eyes. "Everything was all cool but he just be riding me a lil bit too hard about who I hang out with. I look at it like this; I'm 18, so I ain't got time for the bull. I'm going to do what I want when I want. I just learned that the main people that preach, be the main ones they do dirt."

"Wow." She said taking it all in. "I feel you." She said. "So how long you been in the game?" She asked.

"Long enough." He answered quickly.

"Oh ok excuse me." She said with an attitude.

"Naw shawty it ain't even like that. I just don't let a lot of people in my business. No matter how fine they are." He said with a smirk.

This nigga really is flirting with me. She thought to herself. She couldn't resist smiling however. "You are so lame." She grinned. "Cute," she admitted. "But lame."

"Oh so you think I'm cute huh? Be careful shawty it might go to my head." He laughed.

"Damn boy does every word out of your mouth have to be shawty?" She spat with a fake attitude.

"My bad ma." He responded.

She rolled her eyes at his words. "You know what, never mind." She said.

"So what do you like to do when you not in school?" He asked her changing the subject.

"Well, I like singing. I love to read, and I write poetry." She informed him.

"Word? So you like a Nina Simone type huh?" He asked with a flirtatious smile.

"Something like that." She answered.

"That's what's up I dig your style shawty." He told her. "I like the fact that you want your own and you about something." He admitted. "Most of the birds that I meet all about paper; mine."

"Well, a bird is exactly what you're going to get it if that's what you put out there. I mean if you keep attracting these chicks that ain't about nothing but getting your money, then that's what you get. Me? I plan on getting my Masters and opening my own practice soon after." Alexis confirmed.

"A woman with goals, that's what's up. So what type of counseling are you going to be doing?" He dug deeper.

"I'm thinking family counseling. Maybe even sex therapy." she teased licking her lips. She smiled at his laugh.

"You think you funny huh?" he joked.

"Well I mean I'm just saying." She responded winking. "But no I'm just kidding. It will probably be family therapy."

"That's what's up. It's good to see that a woman of color can come and be in an industry like counseling and change the dynamic. It's such a stereotype when it comes to Black families and not being close-knit and all being single mother, father nowhere around types." He explained.

Alexis raised her eyebrows in surprise of his statement.

"What u we're surprised that I dropped knowledge the way I did? Just because I'm in the game don't mean I'm not smart." He said with a laugh.

"I mean damn I guess I just wasn't expecting you to say that." Alexis admitted. "But that's a good thing. Now with you being in the game, is this something that you're going to be doing long term? Are you trying to live up to your father's legacy or something?"

"Nah nothing like that. I'm definitely not trying to be my father. If anything I'm trying to prove that I am NOT him. That's all I ever hear. But at the end of the day, I'm a man and I gotta do what I gotta do. I plan on being out of Georgia in a year, and off in LA building my own empire." He beamed.

Alexis shook her head up and down. "That's definitely a way to go. Good luck with that." She wished.

The waitress came with their food and the two begin to eat. "This is good." Alexis admitted. She ordered her favorite foods, pork chops, macaroni and cheese, pinto beans and rice.

"I told you! This is one of the best soul food spots in Georgia." He bragged. "I come here all the time. Wait till you try the dessert."

"Man look I can't be putting on all that extra weight." She joked. "They may call this the Peach State, but I ain't trying to be as round as one." She giggled.

"Shawty trust me, you got a long way to go before you get that." He mused.

"Oh really?" Alexis asked.

"Hell yea. You thick girl. I mean this may sound real messed up, especially right now but, I was peeping you that day in church. I wanted to say something, but you was catching a lot of people's attention." He informed her.

"I noticed." She laughed. "It's amazing how many elderly men and lay speakers and deacons was trying to get me." She giggled. "Getting attacked by the Geritol crew." she joked.

"Hey can you blame them? Hell. You better be glad a nigga like me trying to be respectful right now. Cause the real nigga in me want to take you back to the crib and bang your back out. But given the situation, I'm chillin." He confessed. "That may sound real fucked up, but shawty it's just something about you that I ain't gonna front, I can't ignore it."

"I'm flattered at your boldness. I guess I could say the same thing." Alexis said. *What the fuck am I saying?* She thought to herself. *I can't stop be saying this shit to him!*

Quinton sit back shocked. "Word?" He asked. "Well shawty you know we can get that dessert to go, and we can go hang out of my crib for a bit. I don't stay far from here." He rambled.

"Don't you got a girl?" She asked.

"You been in the game this long so I'm pretty sure you got a girl." She argued.

"Damn you know what?" He confessed. "I ain't even gonna lie to you, I got a girl. And we live together."

"See? You tryna bring drama." She snapped immediately turned off.

"Nah nothing like that. Honestly, I forgot looking at you. But you right I do got a girl. But I mean it ain't nothin for me to go get a room." He suggested.

Alexis started thinking about what could happen and changed her mind. Quinton sensed her hesitation.

"You ready for me to take you back?" Quinton mustered up.

"Yeah we can go ahead and start heading back in that direction. I really appreciate you getting me out of that car Quinton." She said. "I was just in such a crazy head space. It's hard because my Nana was such a big part of my world. And I know she wanted the best for me. I've done some things that I'm not proud of, and she will probably be ashamed of me if she knew I did. But she never really just made me feel like I wasn't important you know? She was that one person that I knew would be supportive of me no matter what."

Quinton saw that she was about to cry and grabbed her hand. "Believe it or not, that's my sister for me. With everything going on with me and my family right now, I know that no matter what, if I pick up the phone and call my little sister, she's right there. I mean I got my boys and all but when it comes to family, that's the one that has me no matter what, like your grandmother had you. And this may sound cliché, but your grandmother still here with you. Just not in the physical sense. But I bet you every time you feel that shutter, or you feel like someone else is in the room with you and stuff like that, it's her. She's making her presence known. So just do what you gotta do for you shawty." He told stressed. "At the end of the day, no one else has lived in your shoes, and no one else knows your story."

"Thanks." Alexis half smiled.

"No problem shawty. Come on. Let me get you back to your car."

Alexis stood and Quinton embraced her in a hug. "You know this whole bad boy image that you have going for you is so fake." she joked. "You are as soft as a marshmallow."

"I'm gonna let you have that one." He laughed. "Usually I don't let anybody see this side, but given everything that's going on right now, you caught me on a good day."

"Oh that's what it is?" She asked as the two walked out of the restaurant and Quinton helped her in the car. As Quinton walked around to the driver side, Alexis studied his physique. He was tall and gorgeous, with the darkest chocolate skin. She tried not to stare, but his body was nice. She couldn't get over the fact of how much he looked like his father though.

Quinton got in the driver's side and started the car. "Alright Cinderella time to take you back to your pumpkin." He joked with her.

Alexis let out a low laugh. "I would hardly call a Lexus IS 250 a pumpkin." She bragged.

"Whatever. It ain't got nothing on mine." He said showing off his interior upgrades he had put on the car.

"Ok I'll let you have that." She shot back.

Quinton pulled up to the stoplight waiting on the light to change. Alexis appeared hesitant to speak and Quinton noticed. "What's on your mind shawty?" He asked.

"I'm not ready to go back yet." She replied. "I thought I was but, I don't want to go back. Cause then it becomes real again."

"Well what you want to do?" He asked her. "We can drive around, it's up to you."

"I don't know." Alexis answered. "I'm just not ready to go home yet."

"Aight you, I tell you what," he informed her. "I'm going to take you to one of my favorite spots. I go there when I need to chill."

Alexis shrugged. "That's cool. I don't care. I just don't want to deal with anybody right now."

"Cool shawty. I got you." He said.

He drove through College Park to one of his favorite secluded spots. It was hidden from the main road and you would have to drive down a long dirt trail to get to it. He loved coming to the empty field ever since he was in middle school. No one really knew about the place and he could clear his mind. He pulled into the parking spot and cut his car off.

"What is this place?" Alexis asked.

"Uh, it's a field. You don't know a field when you see one?" he smirked.

"I know it's a field jackass." She responded just as sarcastic. "I meant what was so special about it?"

"Man, this place used to be a school back in the day. It was like one of the first schools built. They tore it down like ten years ago and closed it off but I come down here to get some peace. I found it when I was driving around. My pops showed it to me once when I was younger."

Alexis laughed. "You make it sound like you're 50 years old. You ain't even hit 21 yet."

Quinton looked at her serious. "My age shouldn't matter. It's what I can do."

"And what is that?" She asked.

"Shawty you have no idea the kind of things I can do." He told her in a low growl.

"Hmm. I know your ass is a flirt." Alexis stated matter of a fact. "Every opportunity you get you trying to get some."

"I mean, I'm saying I'm trying to jump your bones right now, but I'm just letting you know what I'm capable of yo." he said staring her down.

"And what is that?" Alexis asked playing along.

"A lot." he answered. "But out of respect for you, I don't want to get into that right now." He pulled back.

Alexis opened the car door and got out walking to the front of the car and leaning against the hood. She closed her eyes and took a few deep breaths. Quinton watched her from the inside of the car fascinated. He didn't know what it was about her, but she definitely had him intrigued. He saw her shoulders heaving up and down and knew that she was crying. He got out of the car and walked to the front and held her.

"I'm so tired." She cried into his arms. "Everything just keeps happening; I'm so tired of it all. Why did he take her?" she asked meekly.

Quinton remained silent and continued to hold her in his arms allowing her to cry. The two remained in an embrace for several minutes. When she pulled back, she looked up at Quinton and he saw a look of pain in her eyes. Looking at her, he felt himself starting to get aroused. He wanted to take away all of her hurt that she was feeling at that time. She looked at him longingly and pushed her face towards his and he obliged her leaning in to kiss her slowly.

Before he reached her lips, he whispered, "Are you sure about this? There's no doubt in my mind that I want you, but I don't want to hurt you or take advantage of you either."

Alexis face softened as the tears flowed. “I know this isn't going to fix anything. But I just don't want to think about anything right now. I just want a few moments where I have no problems. Even if it is brief.”

Quinton silenced her placing his lips on hers kissing her slowly and gently. His tongue played with her lips, and he felt her relax in his embrace. She ran her hands up and down his back as he continued to please her with his mouth. Leaning against the car, he unzipped her jacket revealing the button down blouse that she was wearing. He began to unfasten the buttons trailing kisses as he went. He massaged her breasts and began making circles around her nipples. He sucked them gently as Alexis let out a soft moan.

He placed his hand on her thigh and used his fingers to caress her soft skin. Touching her softly, he explored her body until he found her pearl. He massaged it ever so gently and smiled as Alexis squirmed. He held her hands as he begins to kiss her navel leading down to her warm and wet pussy. He licked her clit flicking his tongue quickly in and out. Alexis hissed with pleasure and tried to use her hands to grab him. Seeing her resist, he only held her tighter.

“Don’t run from it.” He whispered. “Just relax. I got you.” He used her body like a canvas and his tongue was the paintbrush. There wasn't a place on her body that he didn't kiss. With every touch he felt his dick getting harder.

“Oh my Gawd!” Alexis moaned. “Please….”

“Please? Please what?” He asked teasing her.

“Please, don't stop.”

Quinton smiled and placed his head back in between her legs continuing to taste her. He pushed her legs backwards spreading her lips and dove in moving his tongue now rapidly through her walls. He could feel her body tensing up and knew that she could not hold on much longer.

“Oh Gawd!” She cried. “I'm about to cum!”

“Comc for mc shawty.” Quinton urged. “Don't fight it.”

Alexis felt her body explode and Quinton took every opportunity to partake of every drop. He felt her body begin to shake and smiled. He lifted his shirt up revealing his six pack and Alexis trailed her fingers along every crease. He unfastened his pants pulling his dick out. Alexis leaned back against the hood of the warm car and felt him enter her body.

*

Chapter Four

I need to stop, she thought to herself. *I shouldn't be doing this right now. But it feels so good.* She felt Quinton stroking her deep. His massive dick throbbed inside of her pussy. He lay on top of her looking her in the eyes as he stroked her slowly in and out and she whimpered in ecstasy. He leaned down and began to kiss her neck making her body temperature rise. She dug her nails into his back as she watched his hips gyrate while inside of her. He continued to thrust vigorously, his body moving rapid. Still inside of her, he stood up and pulled her to the edge of the car her bottom hanging in mid-air. She wrapped her legs around him and he began to pump harder and faster more aroused as he watched her titties bounce up and down from the rhythm.

"Q!" She screamed. "This is so good." She moaned.

Quinton looked down at her. "That's right baby. I told you I wanted to make you feel good." He said as he continued to thrust.

Alexis squeezed her lips around his dick and grinded her body from the hood of the car.

"Damn shawty." He exclaimed. "I see what you trying to do." He pulled out of her quickly and stood her up.

Her legs felt like rubber, but he bent her over the car and entered her from behind watching her ass bounce up against him. He smacked her ass and listened to her hiss.

"That feel good?" He asked her.

"Yes baby." She answered "Yes!"

He began to pound her and Alexis returned the favor bouncing her ass back against him slapping it against his balls. "Damn your fine ass feels so good right now." He grunted. "You gonna make a nigga bust." He said feeling himself begin to get the urge. But he wasn't ready to come yet. He wanted to enjoy her for just a few more minutes.

He pulled himself out of her grabbing her hands and taking her to the passenger side of the car. He set her down on the seat and stood in front of her placing his massive hard dick in her face. Alexis' eyes grew large from the sight of it, but she was more than willing to reciprocate. She took him in her mouth and began to taste the juices that they both created. She grabbed the shaft of his dick with her hand and started licking him, flicking her tongue against the tip of his dick. She then took all of him in her mouth and bobbed her head up and down sucking and slurping him.

"Shit!" She heard him say. Alexis smiled knowing that she had him ready to come. She continued the rhythm going. The warmth of her mouth mixed with the spit made Quinton's eyes roll. Alexis felt his body begin to tense up and relaxed her jaws so that he could feel himself touching the back of her throat.

"Fuck!" He yelled he picked her up and lifted her leg on to the seat of his car and plunged into her. He pumped so hard and fast that Alexis felt like her body was going to combust. Before he can say anything, he felt Alexis nails dig deeper into his skin and her body begin to shiver.

"I'm coming!" she screamed.

"Me too." He moaned. He shot his load inside of her gritting his teeth and muffling a scream.

Quinton panted trying to catch his breath. Alexis look down at the secretions that were dripping from her legs. He took his tee shirt and handed it to her.

"Here. I don't have any Kleenex or anything." He offered.

"Thanks." Alexis said wiping the inside of her thighs.

Quinton went to the back seat and put a wife beater on. "You okay?" He asked as he noticed she grew considerably quiet.

"Yeah." Alexis answered him. "I just…I know I wasn't supposed to be moving that fast. Up until today, I decided not to be with any man until..."

"Until what?" he asked curious.

"Until I got myself together. Until I had learned to deal with the stuff that's happened." She murmured.

"I don't get it shawty. What was so bad that you had to leave North Carolina?" He questioned.

Alexis shook her head. "It started a couple of years ago. I started dating this guy that I went to school with, and he had a baby mama that was still in love with him. He didn't want her and had pretty much been done with her, and he had custody of their daughter, but the baby momma would try any and everything possible to get back with him. So when she found out we were together, she started doing vindictive type shit. She would slash my tires, bust my windows, all kinds of stuff." She explained. "It turned out that my next door neighbor was her other baby daddy. They had been in a relationship and he had a prison record a mile long. It's like one big cluster fuck of drama." She stopped and took a breath. "Anyway, I met him one day walking my dog and he tried to holla but I rejected him. Long story short, somehow, the two of them found out the connection between me and me ex, and he kidnapped me. Almost every day she would beat me, and he raped me. The only reason I got away is because some shake that he had been messing with popped up at the house and he got mad at her and beat her up too. She called the cops and they showed up catching him off guard. I remember that he locked me in a bathroom with that girl. I fought like there was no tomorrow. I ended up killing her. And they took him into custody and found me in the bathroom bleeding."

"Damn." Was all that Quinton could muster. "Yeah that is some shit to have to get over for real." He confessed.

"That wasn't the worst part." Alexis stopped him. "After that I tried to live a normal life. Everything was fine for a while. He and I got back together and then he graduated and moved. I still had a year left of school so he didn't want us to do the long distance thing. I started dating other guys, and I met a guy that I really cared about and really loved." She gulped feeling a lump in her throat. She began to cry. "Everything started falling apart again. I stopped talking to my best friend because her brother was the nigga that kidnapped me. She didn't tell me until later on because she was scared that we wouldn't be friends anymore. We were already kind of estranged or whatever because she tried to get with me one night. I never got the chance to tell her how sorry I was for blaming her. And then somebody killed Collin, and—and--and I don't know who. But he died because of me! And then I guess you could say I hit rock bottom because I started dating a married man who lied to me. He told me he was getting a divorce from his wife, and I believed him. A few months ago when I went to court to testify against JayShawn, the next thing I know, his wife came into the courtroom and started shooting. She killed JayShawn but she also killed my friend!" Alexis' tears flowed freely.

"So in a matter of a few years, people around me have started dying. And I'm tired of fighting, and looking over my shoulder. Both of my best friends are dead. My boyfriend is gone because somebody hated me so much that they killed him." Alexis cried to Quinton continuing her story when something struck her odd. "Wait a minute!" Alexis stopped.

"What's wrong shawty?" Quinton asked confused.

Alexis began to think about what she just told Quentin. "I don't know but something doesn't seem right." She said. "When Collin disappeared and JayShawn escaped from prison, I got a phone call from some chick that said that she knew who killed my boyfriend. She said that she thought JayShawn was responsible for killing my boyfriend. If I'm not mistaken, the chick that I talked to was the same one that I saw at JayShawn's apartment."

"Okay?" Quinton said not understanding what Alexis was referring to.

That was the chick I saw with Collin on campus! She thought to herself.

"It can't be right." She said out loud.

"What can't be right yo?" He asked her.

Not wanting to jump to conclusions she dismissed it. "Nothing." She brushed him off. "I think I may have something but right now I need to get back to my car quick." She asked with urgency.

"No problem shawty." Quitting told her seeing the rush. The two got in the car and he sped back towards the church to take her to her car. Alexis was on to something and she needed to call the detective quickly to confirm her suspicions.

Alexis had an unsettling feeling but she didn't want to talk about it yet until she had more details.

"Everything okay?" he asked.

"Yea." Alexis mumbled. She shook her head after responding and tried to hold it together. "No, I'm not. I honestly don't know how much more I can take. Look I know I probably sent some very mixed signals today, but getting to know you, you seem like a cool dude. Despite the fact that you pretty much got every female in Atlanta trying to get with you." She joked trying to lighten the mood.

He laughed.

"But I appreciate it. You seem like you're easy to talk to you. Maybe, you should try to be doing this conversation with your dad. Couldn't hurt."" She suggested, switching the attention off of her.

Quinton was getting close to the church. He knew that wasn't going to happen. He didn't want to hurt her feelings so he just told her anything to keep her in a good mood.

"Maybe I will." He said half-heartedly.

She looked at him he could feel that he was lying. He pulled up next to her car and she got ready to get out.

"Seriously Quinton. I'm sure your dad will forgive you. And I'm sure he'll understand especially since he has been in the game before himself. You just gotta do what's good for you. At the end of the day, he's still going to love you no matter what. If you stay in the game, he's still going to be your daddy. If you leave the game, he's still be your daddy. That will never change. So just think about it." She advised.

Quinton just nodded his head. Alexis shook her head and rolled her eyes.

"Thanks for the chat." She said opening the door. "And again, I am so sorry about earlier."

"No problem shorty. Don't sweat it." He told her. "You got my number so hit me if you need me." She said.

"I don't think that will be a good idea. Besides, you know your girl will probably whoop your ass." She joked.

"Very funny." He smiled at her.

Alexis waved and walked back towards her car getting in and cranked the ignition. She watched as Quinton drove off. With everything going on, she knew she would have to do everything in her power to stay out of his way. She wanted to remain drama free and today was the day that she planned to start it. Her sleeping with him was the eye opener. She knew that she would have to see the pastor at her grandmother's funeral, but she was determined to let go of any and everything that would keep her from being a better person. No matter what it took, she was going to start over.

"New life, new me." She said reassuring herself.

*

"The spirit of the Lord God is upon me, because the Lord has anointed me; he has sent me to bring good news to the oppressed, to bind up the brokenhearted, to proclaim liberty to the captives, and release to the prisoners; to proclaim the year of the Lord's favor, and the day of vengeance of our God; to comfort all who mourn; to provide for those who mourn in Zion— to give them a garland instead of ashes, the oil of gladness instead of mourning, the mantle of praise instead of a faint spirit. They will be called oaks of righteousness, the planting of the Lord, to display his glory."

Bishop looked out amongst everyone in the congregation at the funeral. He saw Alexis and made it point to stay out of eye shot.

"Now although our dear sister is no longer here in the physical sense, we know that she is still here in spirit just as Christ is still upon us. She touched so many lives here and we have to remember to carry that with us every day that we mourn the dear life of sister Beece. Her granddaughter, Alexis is going to come and bless us with a few words in memory of her. Sister Thomas." He called.

Alexis stood to walk up to the pulpit with a tear stained face. Walking up the aisle a few male members of the congregation gawked at her but Alexis barely knew that they were there. Even in basic attire, Alexis was beautiful. She wore a black pencil skirt with a white ruffled blouse and black stiletto pumps. She wore the pearls that her grandmother bought for her when she turned thirteen.

"Every young lady should own a pair of pearls." She could hear her grandmother tell her.

Alexis stood at the front of the congregation behind the pulpit and looked out at everyone looking at her. She saw all the people that were affected by her grandmother in some kind of way. She stood there speechless for a few moments and stared.

"Um..." she whispered.

She looked to her father who was watching her and trying to fight back the tears that wanted to escape his eyes. She looked around the room and spotted Quinton sitting with who she assumed was his girlfriend. He nodded at her and she quickly looked down. She cleared her throat and began to speak.

"I want to thank everyone for being here today. Seeing how many of you loved my grandmother, it, it really means a lot. My nana used to always tell me that you can know how you are loved by the company you keep. And I see that looking out at you all today, my nana was definitely loved." She wiped her eyes and continued. "My grandmother was the kind of woman that you either really loved, or you really hated. You really loved her because you knew that no matter what, she had your back. And you really hated her because, she always told you the truth even when you didn't want to hear it. I think it was the kids though mostly cause she could catch you with a switch." She joked.

A few members of the congregation chuckled and she saw her father smile.

"But one thing about nana is that she was the type of woman that was a mother to all. There were so many days when my own mother didn't even acknowledge me and I didn't even worry because I knew my nana was right there. I thank God for her because without her, I honestly don't know where I would be in life." Alexis grew quiet for a moment before she continued. "I remember when I felt like I wanted to give up on life. She wouldn't let me. She snatched me up and told me to keep pushing."

Alexis looked down at the casket where her grandmother lay. "It's going to be hard to keep going now nana." She sniffed. "But I won't disappoint you. Just please keep watching over me." Alexis choked back the words.

She took a deep breath and unfolded the paper that she had. "I wrote something for my grandmother that, I wanted to share with you all. My nana was one of the few people that knows that I write poetry and well, I hope that she's listening."

"Go head child." She heard from the congregation.

One summer day the news was brought to me, and I cried and cried.

As I watched you slowly leave me, and with you my heart died.

You never knew how I felt as you suffered your fate

Hearing those dreadful words that day, I can't help but to replay.

You tried your hardest to stay healthy and strong.

Though I tried to deny it, I knew you didn't have long.

You went out fighting, now that's the woman I knew

No matter how much I say it nana, I will always love you.

In me you gave life and instilled in me morals
As I look back now, I regret all our disagreements and quarrels.
I apologize a thousand times, I wish I could have you back
To keep me grounded and to make sure that I stay on track.
Why he chose for you to leave me, right now I can't understand.
But I know that you're probably right up there
watching over me in that great Promised Land.
And I know you're with Pop Pop, and are happy again
But right now my heart hurts with only a pain that you can mend.
I cry as I write this, and I know its tears of hurt and sorrow
Cause I'll only see you in my dreams, but not when I wake up tomorrow.
Nana it's been so hard, since you let me here alone
But I know I'll see you soon when it's my time to come home.
So Lord if you hear me, please keep her close and never let her part.
Let her now that she is the dedication to my heart.
Nana I miss you more than words can say,
And I know that I will see you again soon someday.
Lord keep her safe and keep her near
Let her know that I still may shed tears.
I know my heart is broken, from the loss of my best friend
Nana this is the type of pain that only you can mend.

So Lord if you hear me, keep her close and never let her part

Let her know that she is the dedication to my heart.

She folded the piece of paper back up and let the tears fall. "Thank you." She whispered as she stepped down from the pulpit. She walked back to the pew and sat next to her father where she let it all out.

*

"For the fate of the sons of men and the fate of beasts is the same. As one dies so dies the other; indeed, they all have the same breath and there is no advantage for man over beast, for all is vanity. All go to the same place. All came from the dust and all return to the dust." Bishop recited as he stood atop the platform at the cemetery.

Everyone stood around or sat to observe the burial of her grandmother. As much as Bishop tried to avoid staring at her, he couldn't help but sneak glances at her. Even in such a sad state she was stunning. He glanced at her as the casket was lowered into the ground. Alexis and her father stepped forward and dropped their single roses into the open grave.

"Bye Nana." Alexis whispered.

Her father squeezed her hand and hugged her.

"It's going to be okay." He told her.

Alexis held onto her father feeling security that she had not felt in a while.

"I love you daddy." She whispered.

"Love you too baby girl." He replied.

The two separated and her father looked down at his hurting daughter.

"I'm going to go speak to a few of mama's friends. I'll be back in a few minutes." He said.

"Okay." Alexis agreed.

Her father walked off towards the elders of the church that worked with her grandmother and she turned back towards the grave. She stood there silent until a voice startled her.

"You okay?"

Alexis jumped and turned to see Quinton standing in front of her.

"Damn you scared me!" she exclaimed.

"My bad." Quinton apologized. "I just wanted to come holla at you before I dipped to make sure that you're good." He told her.

"Oh." She said calming her nerves. "I mean I'll be okay I guess." She told him. "I can't say that I can get over it but, all I can do at this point, is live each day like I should. I'm going to make my nana proud of me." She told him.

"I feel you." He said. "I know she probably already proud shawty."

The two continued with small talk and Alexis looked up to see her father looking in her direction. The look he gave her was a look that told her that he needed her to come save him from the ladies that were consuming his time. She smirked and got ready to head in his direction when she looked past him and thought she saw a familiar face. She froze and stared. *I know that's not who I think it is*, she thought.

"Yo!" she heard Quinton call.

"Huh?" she answered snapping out of it.

"I was asking you if you needed anything." He informed her. "Yo shorty you good?" He asked her.

Alexis looked confused. "Yeah. I thought I saw somebody that I knew."

"Okay?" He asked still not understanding what she was talking about.

“Naw I thought I saw this chick that live in Greensboro. Last time I saw her, she was at the trial.” She informed him.

“Okay so is she from Atlanta or something?” He asked. He looked over in the direction she was looking. “I don’t see nobody.”

Alexis looked confused. “I could have sworn I just saw her.” She looked over again to see if she could locate her. She shrugged her shoulders and turned her attention back to Quinton.

“You better get out of here. I don't want you getting in any kind of trouble. Besides, I know my dad will be coming back soon and I definitely don't want to give him the idea that anything is happening.” She told him.

“I got you shorty. I’m on my way to handle some business.” He responded. “Like I said, I just wanted to make sure you was good. Holler at me if you need me.”

“I appreciate it.” She told him.

Quinton gave her a quick hug and began to walk back to his car. Alexis turned her attention back to her grandmothers freshly dug grave.

“I know Nana.” She said out loud. “Trust me I will make sure that I focus on me and do what I'm supposed to do. No more drama. I’m going to make sure that I finish school and do what will make you proud.” She said. “I love you Nana.” She said.

She turned to walk towards her father who was now headed in her direction.

“You ok?” he asked her.

Alexis smiled. “Yep.” She answered. “I’m as good as I can be right now. But, I think I'll be okay.” She said with certain assurance.

Her father looked at her and saw that she was sincere. “I'm glad.” He smiled.

He and his daughter walked towards the car to take them back to the church. Alexis felt confident, but she couldn't shake the feeling that she was being watched.

*

“Shit!” Ariane slid in the seat to make sure that nobody saw her. She sat in the cemetery in a dark Nissan Altima that she had rented watching Alexis across the street. She been following her the last few days learning her routine. She didn't know how she planned to get her back, but she knew that it had to be vicious and torturous. *That bitch needs to suffer. She can't just destroy my life and move the fuck on like everything is okay.* She thought to herself. *I need to be done with her ass once and for all.*

She had planned to just grab Alexis and torture her for a few hours then dump her body, but the more than she thought about it, the more that she wanted her to suffer. So she wanted to learn her routine as much as possible. That way no one would become too suspicious. She had made that mistake with Collin. This time she wanted to do things differently. She wanted to get under her skin. She had already befriended her in Greensboro so she knew that she would be suspicious if she saw her in Atlanta. Thinking about it, she realized she made a mistake coming to the funeral. It was too close and too soon. She had to figure out how she could run into her and not make it look as if she was stalking her.

So far, since she started following her, Alexis was pretty much sticking to herself so she knew it would be easy to get her alone. The only time she ever saw her with anybody was when she was with her grandmother or at the church. She was surprised when she watched her and some boy fucking outside on his car. That was the most action she had seen from Alexis since she got to Atlanta. She wasn't surprised though. *Once a hoe, always a hoe.* She thought. She looked to see if anyone had noticed that she was parked and watching. She looked at the driver's seat and it appeared as if everyone was gone. Relaxing, she got ready to start her car.

Tap! Tap! Tap! She squealed almost jumping out of her skin. Her heart racing a mile a minute, she saw a handsome and attractive black guy at her window. She rolled the window down unable to ignore him and feigned ignorance.

"Yes?" She asked.

"You lost or something?" He asked.

"No." She answered. "I was just taking a minute to get myself together. I was coming to visit my brother's grave." She rattled off.

The boy looked at her skeptical but didn't push. "Okay."

"I'm sorry," she said cutting him off. "Was I bothering you or something?"

"No you're not bothering me sweetheart." He told her. "I was just making sure you was good. Cause it kinda look like you was peeping on the low." He said motioning towards Alexis and her father walking off in the distance. "I mean shit, if I saw something that looked like that too, I would be peeping." He joked. "Shawty bad as hell."

Ariane rolled her eyes and sucked her teeth. “Whatever.” She mumbled.

“So you was peeping?” He repeated.

She tried to act innocent. “I don't know what you're talking about.” She said.

“Now come on girl.” he said. “Clearly your attitude is saying something different. So, what’s good? I know you not the FEDS or nothing like that.” He stated.

Ariane was getting tired of him and she was ready to go. “No it's nothing like that.” She huffed. “I thought I knew the girl but I didn't want to just go up to her. Obviously this isn’t the type of place where you can just go up and question somebody.” she explained. “And if I was wrong in my assumption, I didn't want to be embarrassed. I mean what the fuck I look like walking up to somebody in a cemetery and saying ‘hey do I know you from somewhere?” She snapped at him.

“Chill shorty. Not that serious. Like I said, you was over here in the car and you look like you was kinda hidden from some folks. That's all.” He bargained.

“Well thank you for checking on me, but like I said, I'm fine.” She told him. “Now if you'll excuse me, I need to go ahead and go home.” She said cranking her car.

The boy shrugged her off and Ariane rolled up her window. She pulled out of the parking spot and drove toward the exit.

“Damn it.” She said out loud.

She sighed thinking about the story that she just gave. She looked in the rearview mirror to see him walking towards a group of guys and a black Bentley.

“Definitely gotta be more careful.” She told herself.

She decided to head to her house to regroup on what her next move would be. She didn't have much time, so she had to come up with a plan and fast. She felt tears forming in her eyes. She wanted her life back. She wanted her man back. She wanted the family that they were supposed to have. And she knew she could have neither one of those. But if she was going to be miserable, then so was Alexis.

*

"Did you find out who it was?" Quinton asked.

"Not exactly." His friend answered. "But she definitely was watching. She seemed a little shook. When I asked her was she good, she said she was here to see her brother but she never got out the car." He informed him.

Quinton shook his head in understanding. "Yeah when I was talking to shorty a little bit ago, she said she thought she saw some chick that she knew from back home."

"But my question is, why would she be here at the funeral? I mean does the girl got beef or something?" His friend asked.

Quinton shrugged. "Yo your guess is better than mine my nigga." He said. "I don't even know shorty like that." He answered. "But I mean she seem cool. But you know how females get. If one chick look a certain way or something like that they trip the hell out. My girl the same way. She saw me hugging my cousin and she went the fuck off." He joked. "You know these chicks be getting mad over every little thing." He said.

"True." His friend laughed. "I say just leave it alone."

"Word." Quinton answered. "I'm sure she good." He said.

He played it off but he knew that he wanted to keep an eye on Alexis. He has had her on his mind for the last couple of days. Even though he knew he had a girlfriend, it was something about her that always distracted him. He felt his phone ringing in his pocket. He pulled his phone out to see his girlfriend's name pop up on the screen.

"Yo I swear shorty got ESP or something." He laughed turning his phone around to show his boys her name flashing on the screen. "Hey let me call you back when I get to the car." He told her hanging up the phone. He didn't feel like talking to her at that moment, so he decided to call her when he got home. He mind was too busy at that moment thinking about Alexis.

*

Chapter Five

Alexis walked out of her internship from the hospital and headed towards the elevator. She had been hard at work studying old cases and before she knew it was past ten o'clock. She had parked on the bottom floor earlier that day and was now waiting on the elevator to arrive to the ninth floor of the parking deck. The elevator doors opened and Alexis got on ready to go home and call it a night.

For the last month since her grandmother's funeral, Alexis had thrown herself into class and her internship and was more than exhausted; especially the last couple of days. She had been working multiple hours at the hospital and trying to study for finals. And to make matters worse she had a stomach bug that was slowing her down that night. When the elevator doors opened up to the bottom floor she walked to her car while trying to find her keys. She could hear her heels clicking against the pavement as she walked towards her car in the now almost empty parking lot. A strange feeling came over her as she continued to her car. She quickened her pace and got in.

Closing the door quickly she started her car and drove out of the parking lot. She didn't see anybody, but she felt like she was not by herself. She drove home and tried to shake the nervous feeling that was overpowering her blaming it on paranoia. Speeding home, she made it home in ten minutes flat. Rushing to the door Alexis couldn't contain herself any longer and threw up. Rinsing her mouth out, she lay down on her couch to try to get herself together. *Damn what the hell did I eat?* She thought to herself. She went to her kitchen and made herself some tea to calm her stomach. Lying back down, she turned her television on and watched until she fell asleep.

Alexis woke up at 4:30 in the morning to her stomach upset rushing to the bathroom again.

"Damn it!" She fussed.

She thought about calling her father because she knew she needed to go to the hospital, but she didn't want to wake him up so early. Picking up her phone, she scrolled through her contacts to see who she could call. She had made a few friends since starting Clark Atlanta, but none of them she would consider calling at 4:30 in the morning for help. She grimaced and called the one person that she knew would come and help. She blocked her phone number before calling him just in case his girlfriend was with him. Surprisingly, he answered after the first ring.

"Yo?" He answered.

"Hey." she responded still startled. "Sorry to call you so early this is Alexis." She said.

"Oh hey what's up?" He said changing his tone.

"I'm not bothering you I hope?" She asked.

"You good. I was just up whooping my boy ass on this game." he rambled. "What's up? You changed your mind and want me to visit?" he laughed.

Alexis rolled her eyes. “Yea, no. Is there any way you can do me a favor though?” She asked.

“What you need?” He asked.

“I've been feeling real sick since last night.” She told him.

He stopped laughing when he heard her. “For real? What's the matter?” He asked her.

“I'm not sure. I think it’s just something I ate. I just don't want to risk driving my car and getting sick again.” She explained.

“Oh so you gonna get sick in my car?” he asked.

“No! No I didn’t mean it like that. I meant…”

“It’s okay I’m just messing with you.” He laughed. “So you need me to take you to the hospital?”

“Yeah. If you don't mind. I know it's late, and I don't want to get you in trouble or whatever.” She apologized.

“Relax. Trust me if I was in trouble, don’t you think I would have gotten off the phone by now? Or not even answered.” He suggested.

“I guess.” She admitted.

“But yea I can get you. You definitely don't need to be driving if you sick like that. So shoot me your address and I'll head that way.” He told her.

“Okay.” She said.

She hung up the phone and sent him a text with her address. She got up and went to take a shower and change clothes. Standing in the shower letting the hot water hit her body, she felt relief for a few moments. The minute that she got out, it felt as if her body was on fire. She rushed to put her clothes on and lay back down on the couch to wait for Quinton to pick her up. Within minutes, she heard her phone go off indicating that she had a text message.

Q: I'm outside.

She grabbed her purse making sure that she had her ID and insurance card and walked out the door, locking up behind her. She walked outside to see Quinton waiting in a black Mercedes. He got out of the driver side to open up the door for Alexis to get in. He noticed her face as he closed the door behind her and rushed to the driver side.

"You okay?" He asked.

"I don't know." she answered laying her head against the window. "The last few days my stomach has been hurting, but I just figured it was something I ate. Then when I got home last night I started getting sick and started throwing up."

"Well do you remember eating anything that didn't taste right or something?" He asked her.

"No." She said. "Just the normal. I mean I had something to drink a few nights ago, but I don't think it would cause all this. But whatever it is, it hurts like hell right now." She admitted.

Quinton nodded his head and drove as quickly as he could. Alexis noticed the change in speed.

"It's okay Quinton." she said. "You don't have to speed. I'm not going to throw up or anything like that." She promised.

"I'm not worried about that." He told her. "I just don't want you to have to be in pain too long." He said and slowed down slightly.

He didn't mind driving fast to get her to the hospital, but he knew that he was risking getting pulled over at five o'clock in the morning in a black Mercedes with product in his trunk. He pulled into the hospital parking lot driving to the emergency entrance. He turned his hazards on and opened the door so that she could have curbside service.

"Thanks." She said getting out of the vehicle.

"No problem. I'll be in in a second." He said.

Alexis turned around and looked at him in disbelief. "No it's ok." she argued. "You don't need to go in with me. I'll be fine."

"Not negotiable." he told her. "It's five o'clock in the morning and I'm not gonna leave you here by yourself." He argued.

"Quinton please it's not that serious." Alexis disagreed. "Worst case I can call my dad."

"Well, I wouldn't suggest calling your daddy at five o'clock in the morning until you find out what's going on. So just go inside and I'll be in in a minute." He instructed her.

Not feeling up to questioning him, Alexis just stood there.

"Just go sign in so we can figure out what the problem is. And if you're here that long, then you can call your dad. If not if you're only going to be here for a short amount of time, there's no point in waking him up when I can just take you back home." He reasoned with her. He got in his car leaving Alexis there with her mouth open and drove to the parking area to find a spot.

Alexis sighed and walked inside to register so that she could be seen. She sat down in the waiting room, and pulled her iPad out so that she could catch up on some reading. She loved reading books from Amazon and had not had much opportunity lately because of her schedule. She downloaded La'Tonya West's 'Love and Paper' and began to read. The sliding doors opened a few minutes later and she looked up to see Quinton walk through the door. He looked around and spotted her and came to sit next to her. He had a blanket wrapped around his arm he offered to her, which she took.

"You registered and everything?" He asked.

“Yeah.” she said shaking her head not looking up from her reading.

“That's what's up.” He noticed her attention in the iPad. “So what you reading?” He asked her.

“Love and Paper by La’Tonya West.” She told him

“Oh yea?” He asked. “My girl be reading those kind of books. I don’t see how y'all can get into them.” He laughed.

Alexis looked at him and gave a smile. “Trust me, I can relate to some of these stories. But, above anything else, it’s good reading. So, don't knock it until you try it. Hell I don’t see how yal can be into video games all day long. Y'all got to have the next Madden and it ain't no different than the one that came out the year before.” She pointed out.

“Touché.” He agreed.

“Alexis Thomas?”

Alexis looked up to see a nurse waiting for her at the door. She and Quinton both stood up and Alexis turned to look at him yet again in disbelief.

“I don't even know why you looking like that.” he said. “I told you, I was gonna make sure you're good.”

Alexis shook her head and remained quiet. She walked towards the nurse who looked at her with a curious expression.

“Don't you work here?” She asked her.

Alexis shook her head yes. “I intern for the mental health ward.” She told her.

“I knew you looked familiar.” the lady told her. “Come on this way sweetie.” she directed her. “You should have said that when you registered. Then we could have had you back already instead of waiting.” She told her.

"It's okay. I didn't mind it. My stomach has settled a little bit. I actually don't feel as sick anymore. I just wanted to be on the safe side." She told her.

The nurse walked them into an empty room for her to change. "Well you know the drill." the nurse told her. "Go ahead and put this on so we can get you looked at."

"Okay." Alexis told her.

Quinton stayed outside so that Alexis could change into the gown. The nurse walked out and barely glanced at Quinton closing the door behind her. Alexis quickly changed and opened the door a few minutes later and Quinton walked in. He smiled making her uncomfortable.

"What are you smiling about?" She asked.

Quinton looked her up and down. "Even in a hospital gown you're still sexy as hell." He admitted.

Alexis groaned at his comment and lay back on the hospital bed. "I'm not even going to say anything on that." she mumbled.

"My bad." He told her. "Just got to speak the truth. How's your stomach feeling?" He asked her changing the subject.

"I mean it's okay I guess." she said. "It's been hurting but there's nothing I can really do until the doctor comes in."

"Well hopefully they'll be here soon." Quinton told her.

Alexis laughed. "Doubtful. This hospital is slow at night. We going to be in here a while, so you might as well get comfortable." She told him.

She turned her iPad back on and continued reading the book she had started earlier. Quinton set back in his chair and put his phone out and started playing games. She noticed how focused he was.

"What are you over there doing?" She asked.

"Playing chess." He answered.

"Shut up. You play chess?" She asked.

"Yeah why you say it like that?" He asked her.

"I mean I just didn't really see you as a chess player." she admitted.

"The way I see it, you can learn a lot playing the game. The game of chess is how you play in life. So I play to win." He said focusing back on the game.

The nurse tapped on the door and came in. "Hey Miss lady." She greeted her. "I'm Tiffany, I'm going to be your nurse tonight. Alright so tell me what's been going on." she requested.

Alexis began telling her why she was there. "Well basically I started throwing up last night. My stomach has been bothering me the last couple of days but I just figured it was something that I ate. So I just wanted to see if it was food poisoning or not."

"Okay." Tiffany responded. "Let's go ahead and get some blood work and then I need you to pee in this cup for me real quick." She told her handing her the clear container.

Alexis took the cup from her hand and walked to the bathroom that was attached to the room.

"Just stick it in the little box in there and we'll go have it sent off for lab work." Tiffany instructed her.

"Ok." Alexis went in to the bathroom and filled the cup sticking into the box for the technicians to take to the lab. She came back out and sat on the bed waiting for the nurse to draw a few vials of blood.

"You need me to step out?" Quinton asked standing.

"Now you want to give me some privacy?" Alexis laughed.

"Whatever shorty." Quinton said sitting back down and paying attention to his game.

Alexis sat still while the nurse began to prep her to draw blood. She could smell Tiffany's perfume and the nauseous feeling overpowered her. Alexis swallowed hard to prevent herself from vomiting.

"You okay?" Tiffany asked drawing the last vial.

"Yea." Alexis answered a few moments later. "I'm good. She said.

Tiffany placed the cap on the bottle and stuck them in the carrier.

"Okay I'm going to send the stuff off and we should get something back in about an hour". She told her.

"Thank you." Alexis answered lying back down on the bed.

She pulled the blanket over her body and curled up in it closing her eyes. Seeing her resting, the nurse tiptoed out of the room turning the light down so that Alexis could get her sleep.

"I'll be back to check on you in a few." She told her before she closed the door.

Quinton lay his head against the wall closing his eyes. Instantly, Alexis fell asleep. About an hour later, Alexis woke up to the nurse knocking on the door and saw that Quinton had moved from the wall to the end of the bed.

"Come in." she whispered.

"Sorry to wake you." Tiffany said walking into the room. "We got your lab results back."

Quinton, hearing the nurse sat up to find out what they knew.

"Okay, so what's the deal?" Alexis asked.

"Well um, it's not food poisoning." the nurse told her.

"Well then what else could it be? Stomach bug? What?" Alexis asked.

The nurse fidgeted looking at Alexis. “Looks to be that you’re about five weeks pregnant.” She informed her.

Alexis felt all the color drain from her face.

“What?” She asked in disbelief. “Wait, what?” She repeated.

“We did a pregnancy test with your urine. You know any time we ask for a urine sample we have to do a pregnancy test just to make sure. Well the pregnancy test came back positive so we took a sample from the blood work and based off your HCG levels in the lab results, it came back that you're about five weeks pregnant.” the nurse explained.

Quinton shocked, sat and looked between the nurse and Alexis.

“That's impossible.” Alexis exclaimed. “My period comes like clockwork.” She snapped.

“I understand.” the nurse told her. “When was the last time that you got your period?”

Alexis thought back. “Last month. I got it on the thirteenth.” She told her.

“The thirteenth of May?” The nurse asked her.

“Yeah.” She answered.

“Well sweetie it's June 29th.” The nurse hesitantly told her.

Alexis froze and listened to what the nurse was telling her. “This just can't be fucking right.” She mumbled. “Pregnant?” She repeated.

Quinton’s eyes were dancing and Alexis mind was racing a mile a minute. Quinton cleared his throat and spoke to the nurse.

“Can you give us a minute please?” He asked.

“Sure.” the nurse complied nervously rushing out of the room.

“Are you okay?” He asked her.

“No!” She hissed. “No I'm not ok. I can't be pregnant, I just can't be. I can't!” She repeated.

“Okay you gotta calm down for real.” Quinton told her. “I understand that you're upset right now, but you really gotta relax. Now, just take a couple of deep breaths.”

Alexis was to wound up to hear what Quinton was saying.

“This shit is not for real. I can't afford to be pregnant right now. I've got school, I've got work, I'm damn near finished with my first year of grad school. I gotta be on my grind right now. I can't be trying to have babies and stuff. She rambled. Five weeks pregnant?” She said out loud.

Quinton stood up and walked in front of her so that she could see him. “Alexis, chill the fuck out for a minute. Now I hear everything that you're saying, but you getting yourself worked up right now.”

He pulled the stool that was at the edge of the bed to sit directly in front of her. Alexis begins to cry.

“I can't be pregnant Quinton!” she wept.

She cried heavily and Quinton not used to all the emotions tried to comfort her.

“My dad is going to be so disappointed in me.” She cried. “He’s gonna kill me.”

“It’s alright shorty. You know I got you. If you need me to help talk to him I will.”

Alexis looked up at him completely confused. “What? Why?” She asked.

"Well if I'm not mistaken, the nurse said you were five weeks pregnant." He reminded her. "And about a month and some change ago, we had our little situation. And I know I may not be in school and everything, and I may not have gone to college, but I damn sure know how a baby is made." He said.

Alexis felt everything in her stomach rising at that moment. Quinton noticed her expression and grabbed the trash can that sat next to the bed as she threw up whatever was left in her stomach. Alexis could barely think straight. She didn't know what to do, but her mind was telling her that she was in for a world of trouble. *He thinks that this is his baby*, she thought to herself. *How do I know for sure if he is when I fucked his father the same damn day?* Thinking about it only made her cry harder.

"It's alright." She heard Quinton say. "I got you." He promised her.

Alexis sniffed and removed herself from his embrace. "I need you to just give me some room to breathe." Alexis told him. "Please, just give me some room."

Quinton backed away from her pissed but not saying anything. He was starting to get irritated because she was all over the place and taking it out on him.

"Look Quinton," she started. "All of this right now, it's just going really fast for me and I need some time to think." She told him.

"Think about what?" Quinton asked her. "I know you not about to go do nothing stupid." he argued. "I mean damn I am standing right here." He spat.

"I didn't say that Quinton." Alexis retorted. "I'm just saying that I just fuckin found out that my ass is pregnant. I need you to just give me a fuckin minute to think." She hissed. "Please. Just give me some time to think about how I'm going to at least tell my father that his daughter is pregnant." She pleaded.

"Ok." Quinton agreed. "I'm not trying to push you into doing nothing shorty, that's not my style. I just don't want you to go do something that you will regret later. Especially if you think that is going to be to make my situation better or something like that. I see niggas do stuff like that all the time getting they girls to have abortions and shit, or just not taking care of their shorties but that ain't me." He explained. "So I was just letting you know that I wasn't one of these other niggas that was out here."

"Ok." She sighed. "I understand. I'm just saying to give me a couple of days to try to figure some stuff out. My dad is not an easy person, and I don't want to just spring this on him in the wrong way." Alexis said.

"I feel you. Well," he said changing the subject, "Let me go ahead and get you home. I'm going to go ahead and go get the car so that way you can get dressed. Meet you out front?" He asked.

Alexis nodded her head and Quinton walked out the door.

"Fuck!" She said to herself.

She couldn't believe that this was happening to her. The nurse walked back in the room as she was putting on her shoes.

"Everything okay?" She asked.

"No." Alexis answered after staring at the woman that advised her of her trouble. "Nothing is okay right now. And I seriously don't think that it will ever be okay again." She grabbed her bag and stormed out of the room unsure of what lay ahead of her.

*

Alexis lay in her bed for the third day in a row contemplating how she was going to tell her father that she was pregnant. She has been locked away in the house aside from going to work, and doing everything in her power to avoid Quinton. He had texted her a couple of times to check on her but she was not responding. She knew that it was only a matter of time before she would have to talk to him, but her main priority with her father. *I can't believe that shit keeps getting worse,* She thought to herself.

She had nobody to blame but herself. Even though she was on the path to becoming a better person, her past kept haunting her. She sent her father a text inviting him over for dinner and let him know that she had some exciting news. She knew that she had to be honest with him. *At this point hell it's not like I could do any worse.* She didn't know exactly how to feel with being pregnant, but she knew that she had to figure some things out. Starting with finding out who the father was. She figured that her father would be disappointed for the simple fact that he wanted better for her.

Her mother had her when she was eighteen and in college and had to drop out. Even after her mother gave her away, all she ever heard was that he didn't want her to end up like her mother. Alexis had not seen her mother in ages but she always promised herself that she would do better. She had lived most of her life aiming to set goals and break barriers that her parents couldn't. She was the first one in her family to graduate college, and even though she had a very rocky past, she was not an unwed teenage mother. Hearing that she was pregnant was something she just could not handle. *I mean well, I do still have time to have an abortion,* she thought. She quickly dismissed that idea from her head. Even though she knew she wasn't ready to be a parent, she knew abortion wouldn't be the way to go either. She wanted to call the bishop to let him know, but she was scared of the risk of the situation getting any worse than what it already was. Feeling emotional, she broke down in tears.

Her phone rang and she looked down to see a number she did not recognize. She saw the 336 area code and knew that it had to be from her hometown.

"Hello?" She answered sniffling.

"Hey girl!" She heard a girl greet her.

"Hey." Alexis answered unsure. "Who is this?" She asked.

"It's me. Ariane. I know it's been a minute since you heard from me". She said.

Alexis frowned. Last time she saw Ariane or even spoke to her she was in the courtroom at JayShawn's trial after he had been caught. Even then her attitude around her was a little off.

"Yes it's been a minute." She said. "Like over a year ago." She snapped. "So what's up?"

Ariane caught the attitude in her tone. “Well damn. My bad I didn't mean to bother you. I was just calling to see how you were doing. I know it’s been a minute and I know you had gone through a lot so I was just checking on you.” She said. “Excuse the hell out of me.”

Alexis calmed down and apologized. “My bad. I just got some shit going on right now. I'm sorry I really didn't mean to be rude girl.” She said.

Ariane laughed it off. “It's okay. I'm just glad that you are doing good. Shoot I’m trying to get adjusted my damn self. I just moved to Atlanta a couple of weeks ago to live out here with my brother. He didn't want me in Greensboro by myself; especially after everything happened.” She told her.

Alexis thought back to her grandmother’s funeral a few months prior and thought about how she was unsure of if she saw her or not. She was starting to get that uneasy feeling again.

“I feel you.” She said half-heartedly not wanting to say anything.

She still had her suspicions about the girl, but she was going to make sure to check her at her own pace. She didn't want to scare her off, so she had to play it smart. The more she thought about it the happier she was that Ariane reached out. She had a feeling that she was involved in her troubles more than she let on.

“So what's up girl? Why did you decide to move to Atlanta?” Alexis asked.

“Well like I said my brother didn't want me in Greensboro anymore by myself, so he invited me to come live with him and his wife. It was nothing in Greensboro for me anymore so, I figured I might as well.” Ariane told her.

"Yea it sucks when your life is turned upside down because of some mess." Alexis said with a hint of sarcasm. "So what you need?" She asked.

Ariane sat in silence for a few seconds. "Look," she started. "The main reason I was calling you is because I really wanted to apologize for everything that happened. I know the first time that you met me it wasn't really on a positive note and I know I was a complete bitch." She admitted. "But JayShawn played my ass and had me thinking that he really gave a damn about me. If you had only known half the stuff that he was telling me about you. That's why I didn't like you. And then when everything went down, and I found out he was with that other bitch"

"Oh you mean the bitch that fucking tried to kill my ass?" Alexis snapped cutting her off.

"Yeah." Ariane answered. "I mean I don't know the girl. So trust me it's not like I had anything to do with it. It just pissed me off that JayShawn could do something like that. He fucked around on me with this bitch but telling me that he love me and want to be with me. I put up with him through so much shit, and he just did my ass fuckin dirty. Giving this nigga money, only to find out he had a baby by her. And I know when I called you, I probably came off real crazy and shit but that's not what it was. I just wanted him to feel what I felt. I didn't know that he was involved with all that other shit. I just found out and I couldn't keep it a secret. I couldn't carry that guilt." She started crying.

Alexis sat silent on the other end. "Tell you what," she suggested. "Why don't we meet up for lunch or something?" She asked her. "This way we can talk in person and get it all out."

Ariane sniffed and Alexis could tell that she was surprised. "For real?" She asked "Wow yea I guess so. I mean I don't want you to just be wanting to go out or anything out of pity." she told her.

"Nah" Alexis disagreed. "You're good. So since you're new in town how about you let me know when to come pick you up and I'll take you to this banging soul food spot?" She asked her.

"Okay." Ariane agreed excited. "When did you want to go?" She asked.

"How about tomorrow?" She asked her. "I got a light schedule and I'm off from my internship so I have a little bit more free time."

"Okay cool!" Ariane said. "I will shoot you my address and then I'll see you then." She told her.

Alexis rushed her off the phone. "I'll hit you up tomorrow. Let me go ahead and go cause I got to start studying for this exam." She lied.

"Oh my bad. Yea girl go ahead." Ariane replied.

"Aight, talk to you later." Alexis ended hanging up the phone. She leaned back on her couch and thought about the conversation they had. Something wasn't sitting right with her as far as Ariane was concerned and she was determined to get to the bottom of it. The fact that she popped up in Atlanta and claimed that she was moving there and happened to call her didn't add up, and Alexis was not going to allow herself to be surprised by anymore bullshit. She needed help and knew just who to call. She had to get in touch with Quinton but she didn't know if he was with his girl or not.

She blocked her phone number and called his phone letting it ring twice and then hanging up worried that his girlfriend would answer. Within a matter of seconds her phone rang and she saw his name appear.

"Hey what's up you just call me?" He asked.

"How'd you know it was me?" She inquired surprised.

"Cause you're the only one that calls me private." He laughed.

"Well I mean damn Quinton you do have a girlfriend. I'm starting to wonder if you still have a girlfriend cause hell it seems like you're never with her. So it ain't no telling what she thinking." Alexis retorted.

"Man ok. She know what the deal is. I ain't got time to be out here dealing with drama and all that clingy stuff." He told her. "Right now I'm out handling business and she understands that. She not going question me every second of the day because hell she know what type of work I do. If anything she do it just as much, so like I said, we got an understanding. What we do is what we do. When we together, we together. But when we not, we ain't worried about what the other is doing. That's how I do it that's how I like it." She said.

"Okay." Alexis conceded.

"What you calling to grill me?" He asked.

"No trust I ain't worried about you like that. Anyway," she said changing the subject. "That's not the reason why I called you. I called you cause I need your help with something."

"What? Everything okay? Are you good?" He rattled off.

"Yeah everything is fine, it's nothing like that." Alexis answered realizing the panic that she had placed in him. "Remember how I told you that I thought I saw somebody from back home a few weeks ago at my grandmother's funeral?" she asked.

"Yeah I think so." he answered. "What's up? What you need?"

"Well, I knew I wasn't tripping. I did see her. She never outright said that she was there at the funeral, but it was definitely her. She called me today and told me that she moved to Atlanta to live with her brother, but I don't believe that. I think that she has something to do with Collin getting killed, cause she used to fuck with that dumb ass nigga JayShawn. Now all of a sudden, she's here in Atlanta? It's too much of a coincidence for me. And I'm sorry but I've been in situations in the past where I've gotten close to people and those people were the ones that hurt me. I'm not about to do that shit again. So if her plan is to get me, I'm going to get her ass first." Alexis said firm.

"Hold up. Shorty right now you can't be doing shit with what you got going on. Look Lex I understand you mad and want to find out what really happened and everything but you need to handle one thing at a time." He told her.

“I am about to handle this!” She exclaimed. “Just because I got this situation as you call it, don't mean that I'm gonna let some bitch get to me. You don't understand what the fuck I've been through these last couple of years Quinton. I have damn near lost every fucking thing. All this stupid ass shit done had me lose my best friend, my fucking boyfriend is fuckin dead, probably because of me too, and the nigga that I thought that I loved I ain’t even talking to all because of his fucking crazy ass baby mama!” she yelled. “So no I'm not going to sit back and just let this shit keep happening to me. If anything I thought you would understand!”

“Okay calm down.” He told her. “Where you at?” He asked.

“I'm at home why does it matter?” She said.

“Alright look I'm bout to come scoop you. This is not some shit that we need to talk about over the phone. I'm gonna come scoop you, we'll go somewhere and chill for a minute and you can let me know what's going on. Like I said I got you. Just calm the hell down because I am NOT trying to deal with no extra shit and I damn sure can't afford to have you caught up right now since you carrying my child.”

Hearing him say that made her shudder. Alexis rushed him off the phone. “Alright just hurry up and get here when you can. Because one way or another, with or without you I ‘ma handle this bitch.” She said through gritted teeth.

“Alright I'm on the way.” He said ignoring her attitude. “I'm in Buckhead right now so it’s going to take me about twenty minutes to get there.” He informed her.

“Alright whatever. I told my Pops to come over for dinner but I'm a call him and just tell him to meet me tomorrow. Because I want to get this shit taken care of first.” She told him.

“Have you told him yet?” he asked curious.

“No that’s why I invited him over so I could break it to him.” She answered. “I really don’t want to talk about that right now.”

“Alright cool baby girl no worries.” He said.

She hung up the phone and jumped out the bed too get dressed.

“This shit going to end now.” Alexis vowed.

*

Chapter Six

Ariane hung up the phone with Alexis and smirked.

"Stupid bitch." She hissed. "I can't wait to get rid of this bitch once and for all."

She smiled at herself and the performance that she put on while on the phone with Alexis. She was running out of options on how to get close to Alexis without her being suspicious so she just decided that she would be honest with her and telling her that she moved to Atlanta. *Who knew the truth would work?* She thought to herself with an evil giggle. She wasn't expecting Alexis to invite her to lunch, but it was all the more better.

She wanted to grab the opportunity to take her out, and this was her chance. Ariane was going to trap Alexis into taking her to an abandoned location she had spotted while out where she was planning to take her and kill her. She loaded up her car with the shovel, tape and everything else that she needed to get rid of Alexis with. She took it to her car and decided to take everything to the house so that way everything will be in place for when she got there. Ariane was perhaps the happiest she had ever been in so much to the point that she was humming.

She opened her closet to see a box sitting in the corner. She slowed down and picked it up to see the pictures of JayShawn that sat inside. It tore at her and she thought about everything that she had lost. Images of JayShawn faded with the thoughts of killing Alexis.

"It's too bad Alexis. You took everything from me. And now, you're going to pay with your life."

*

Alexis sat in the car next to Quinton as she told him her plans.

"Okay so exactly how do you know this chick again?" He asked.

Alexis sighed and repeated herself. "When me and Henderson were together, his baby mama was messing with JayShawn. JayShawn was the guy that I was telling you about. He was my next door neighbor. I didn't really know him like that, but I knew he was like watching me every time I was out. There were a couple of times where I saw him outside with a few of his homeboys and I remember one time when I came outside to my car he was out there with this chick. I swear that she was Ariane. So basically a bunch of shit went down, me and Henderson broke up and I had gone over to JayShawn's house. Turns out this nigga had put some shit in my drink and I remember waking up and being in his bed. His fucking girlfriend, Henderson's crazy ass baby momma was there and these two tortured my ass. Him and his bitch damn near fuckin killed me. Long story short, Ariane's ass saved my life because she came over to JayShawn's house when she found out Keisha was there. They got into it I guess cause I heard her screaming and he hit her."

Quinton listened quiet and intensely as Alexis continued.

"So she called the cops and that's why the cops showed up to his house. Keisha tried to keep me quiet but I ended up stabbing her and killed her in self-defense. They arrested his ass and locked him up, and I pretty much move the fuck on with my life. I still didn't know if she had any connection to this nigga like that. So I started dating Collin and everything was cool for a while. But we ended up breaking up over some stupid shit that I honestly don't even think was important and we didn't talk to each other. One day I saw him on campus with this chick I thought it was her, but this chick was pregnant like I couldn't really tell. The next thing I know I'm hearing that Collin is dead, and this is around the time that JayShawn escaped from prison. So of course I'm freaking the fuck out and trying to figure out what the hell is going on, and then all of a sudden she hits me up out the blue and she tells me that she thinks that dude had something to do with Collin being killed. So long story short, the cops chased his ass down and found him in some damn apartment complex. But the only thing is not making sense to me is how does she know dad it was Collin? Like, I remember she hit me up and told me that she thought he killed my boyfriend. So I'm trying to figure out how she didn't think it was just some random nigga and how she connected it to me. So she's either helping this nigga, or she's doing this shit herself. Either way the shit ain't adding up. So like I said, I'm not going to sit back and just let this shit keep happening. I gotta stop this now."

Quinton listened to everything that she was saying and shook his head.

"Yo this is some really fucked up type shit." He said. "I'm not going to lie to you, I thought my shit was messed up with the bull that I've been through, but I think you got me beat. That was a lot.

"I know." She agreed.

"Let me make sure I got this straight." He said recollecting everything she told him. "So you was fuckin with some nigga who's baby mama was fuckin with your neighbor?"

"Yep." Alexis answered his question.

"And your best friend is buddy's sister and you didn't know about it?" He asked.

"Yep." Alexis told him.

"So this nigga decided that he was going to try to get with you and you told him no, so….he did all of this shit because you rejected him?" He asked.

"No this muthafucka did this shit because he's fuckin sick in the head. Even now that this nigga is dead he's fuckin haunting my ass!" she yelled.

She punched the dashboard out of frustration.

"Yo chill out ma!" He stopped her. "I'm just trying to get understanding of it. Otherwise I wouldn't be here."

Alexis begin to cry at everything that was happening. Quinton drove for a few more minutes until he reached the park. He pulled into the parking lot and cut the ignition off. Alexis was so involved in the story that she wasn't even paying attention to where they were going. She looked up and realized that they were parked and relaxed a little.

"Look, Quinton I'm really not trying to further complicate your life. I swear I'm not. But, for some reason, trouble just seems to find me. I don't go looking for it, I don't ask for it, but every time I turn around, no matter how right I'm trying to be, no matter what I'm trying to do the right way, shit just keeps happening. Ever since I met Henderson, my life has been a living hell. I'm not saying he's to blame for it, because a lot of the shit that I did was really fucked up. But, I just can't shake my past. I've tried I swear I've tried!" She cried.

"I'm not proud of a lot of the things that I did. But I can't take it back, and I refuse to keep being punished for it. That's why I got to stop this shit." She said.

The tears were falling from her face and Quinton listened to her. After a few moments he finally spoke.

"So tell me everything." He said.

"What?" She asked wiping the tears.

"Tell me everything. You said that you had a fucked up past and that a lot of shit happened that you regret. Tell me." He repeated.

"Why?" She asked confused. "I mean what does it matter now?"

"It does." Quinton told her. "Because I think one of the reasons why you're so frustrated is because you haven't really had an opportunity to tell your story to somebody that's not going to judge you. You think that people are judging you because they're finding out in a way that isn't really a way that you want them to. So, tell me. I want to know everything."

Alexis looked at him and shrugged her shoulders. "I mean you pretty much know everything. Well, most of it." She said.

"Ok but most ain't all." He disputed. "So spill."

"Well like I said, it's a lot. My mom pretty much didn't want me, and she gave me up. My dad is like all I have, he's the one that took care of me. Him and my Nana where my parents. They always wanted me to be better than my mother. That's all I ever heard. How I couldn't screw up. So I always had to go above and beyond. I was pretty much good until I got to college. I don't know I guess I just wanted to have fun and not have to worry about people judging me."

"Okay." Quinton acknowledged showing interest.

"Anyway, the last couple of years, let's just say I didn't leave the normal college life. When I got to school, I pretty much wild out or whatever you wanna call it. I did whatever I wanted to do and I really didn't care about what people thought about me. I've never really cared what people thought about me honestly. Maybe that was the problem, I don't know. But, I was always at every party, I was always in the middle of things. I always had guys tryna holla at me. I've never really went too crazy, but a lot of girls hated me because of the fact that I was always getting some niggas attention. A lot of guys knew that I had a reputation, and hell they did just what niggas do."

Damn! Quinton thought. *She for real bout hers.*

Alexis continued. “When I met Henderson, I wasn't really planning on getting in a relationship, but I really was feeling him. He had like this cockiness about him and told me that I was gonna be his girl.” She laughed. “We got together and everything was good. He told me upfront that he had a kid, and I was okay with it. I just didn't know that his baby momma was a fuckin psycho. And I didn't really let it bother me until I met her face to face. When that shit happened to me, it was like a part of me died. I turned my back on the wrong people because of that shit. These motherfuckers kidnapped me and locked me in a fuckin closet. I felt like trash. I mean JayShawn raped me damn near every day and his bitch sat there and took it out on me because of the fact that he was raping me. She would kick me and punch me and do everything to me but there was nothing I could do. So when I did get free I fought back. I fought back and I did something I never thought I could.”

Alexis paused to catch her breath and wipe her face.

“I didn't want to kill her, but I didn't see any other option. When they arrested him, I thought everything was over. I thought everything was good. He was in prison, she was dead, and that was supposed to be it. I mean me and my best friend, me and her weren’t really speaking because of the fact that I thought she had something to do with it.”

“Why would you think that?” He interrupted her.

Alexis sniffed and explained.

"Well one night Tamika came over to my apartment to hang out. And we started drinking and shit and shit went left like real quick we were so drunk. Next thing I know, she's trying to eat my pussy and I'm thrown. She's telling me that she's been in love with me, and she can't figure out why I wanted Henderson, and I told her to leave. I guess I really fucked up because I thought that she was mad at me and I accused her of wanting to get back at me and telling JayShawn where I was. And in retrospect, it was really fucked up of me to think that, and looking back on it now I'm so sorry that I did that shit to her. But I really thought that she was trying to hurt me. So, I stopped talking to her. Even after he got locked up, and she apologized, I just didn't want to speak to her. It was just me and my best friend Summer, and that was it."

"Okay so you just stayed to yourself?" he asked.

"Well, then I met Collin, and we started dating. I didn't really want to date anybody because I thought that they would end up doing the same thing that JayShawn did, or call me a hoe. But I met him and I was happy. And everything was fine until that night that we got into an argument." She remembered.

"Well what was so bad about the argument?" He questioned.

"Nothing! That's the thing." She told him. "We got into argument over Tamika. I told him about how she pissed me off over something that in hindsight was really petty but, at the time, I was so angry. He called me on my shit and told me that I was being selfish and should have just work it out where her. But I didn't want to hear it. He walked out the door, and....and...and I never saw him alive again."

She felt herself getting choked up. “I had seen him on campus one day after all of that went down, but he was with this chick.”

“And this is when you thought you saw the girl?” he asked her.

“Yea!” she exclaimed. “I could have sworn that it was her but, this chick was pregnant and he was too far away for me to see. I called him a couple of times but he never responded. The last time I heard anything was when I ran into his line brother on campus and he was telling me that there was some fire drill or something in be building that he was in for class. A couple of days later, I got a phone call and my friend told me to turn on the news and I saw that they found Collins body in his apartment. So of course I fuckin lost it. And rather than just be by myself and deal with the shit, I jumped right on to another nigga. For a while I was in therapy but, I just stopped going.”

Quinton was in complete amazement at her story.

"So the guy that I started messing with was older and he was married. I don't know what the fuck I was thinking, but he was giving me the attention that I wanted. I'd started to slack off in school, and I was losing it. Then one day Ariane hit me up and told me that she found out that JayShawn was out of prison and that she felt like my life was in danger and that he was trying to kill everybody to get to me. And of course I believed her because I had my windows broken and my car tires would be flattened and all I kept thinking was I'm tired of it." She said. "Next thing I know, me and Summer find out that Tamika was killed. I called the guy I was messing with for help and he got a hotel room for us to stay in because the cops didn't think it was safe for us to go home. Summer had gone to check on Tamika's mom and I had invited him up to the room to keep me company. Why I did that I don't know. And I remember telling him that I didn't want to continue to talk to him because of the fact that he had a wife. He told me that she and him were getting a divorce and he didn't love her anymore and that he was going to be filing for separation and all of that. So I asked him to leave because I figured Summer would be wanting to meet up soon and I get ready to leave the room, and the next thing I know, his wife jumps out and attacks me and tells me that she hired a private investigator and that she knew he had been with me. She damn near killed me and told me that if I didn't stay away from him that she would finish the job. Next thing I know I woke up and I'm in the hospital and my father is there. And it hurt to see the look on his face when he found out that I had been attacked."

"Damn." Quinton whispered. "What did he say about everything?"

"I lied and I didn't tell him that some grown ass woman attacked me because I was fucking her husband. I told him it was random. So around this time and it's time for this nigga JayShawn trial and they told me they needed me there to testify. Before I could even figure out what happened, I'm at the trial and my dad, Henderson and Summer are with me." She said.

"So you and ole buddy got back together?" Quinton interrupted.

"Yea he and I were working it out at that point." Alexis noticed his clenched jaw but didn't mention it. "But during the trial, I look up and see the nigga that I'm fuckin is JayShawn's fuckin attorney! And he is looking at me all funny and shit and basically, all of my business is put out there in the street. Then before I can even have a reaction to it, the courtroom door opens and his wife comes in and she's looking all deranged and crazy and start shooting and bullets were flying everywhere and my best friend ended up getting killed and JayShawn got killed and everybody just started dying all because of me! And I'm having to tell my father and my best friend's mother, that the reason why my best friend is dead is not because of the fact that some crazy bitch came in there shooting at everybody at random. No! It's because of the fact that she came in there looking for me! If I wasn't fuckin her husband, she wouldn't have been trying to kill me!" She screamed. "Everything is all my fault! And I try to apologize to Henderson but he just left! He left me there! And the look of disappointment on my father's face when he found all this out. It was so….so…..so damn embarrassing because the damn detective is sitting here pretty much laughing as he's asking me these questions in front of my father."

Alexis was gasping for air so hard that Quinton thought she was going to hyperventilate. He placed his hand on her back and rubbed her to soothe her.

"Just breathe." He instructed her.

"No, Quinton, you don't get it." Alexis said in between sobs. "It was like he wanted to humiliate me! I was made a joke of. And my father told me he thought it was best that I just leave Greensboro behind me. And I did. And I came here and I made a promise to my grandmother that I was going to do what I was supposed to do, and that I was going to live my life the way I'm supposed to live it. I went back to Greensboro for the trial, and I left that part of me there. I made a promise to my grandmother, and I plan on sticking to it. And then my dumbass goes and does something stupid and now my ass is pregnant."

Quinton frowned when he heard her say that. "So having a baby is stupid?" He asked.

"No Quinton!" She yelled. "I didn't even say that! Don't put words in my mouth. No of course the baby is not stupid. But how I got the baby is." She told him.

Quinton nodded his head but didn't say anything.

"What?!" She asked.

Quinton opened his mouth to speak. "Is that everything?" He asked.

Alexis knew that there was more, but she wasn't ready to tell him quite yet. She didn't want to risk telling him at that time if she didn't need to. Besides, she knew that she needed him to help her get rid of Ariane if she really was dirty.

"Yes." She said after a long pause.

"Okay." He said.

"What do you mean okay?" She asked confused.

“Just what I said. Okay.” He repeated. “Do you feel better?”

“Actually, yea.” She sniffed.

“Now let me make sure that you understand this. I'm not these other niggas that you fucked with.” He told her. “I'm not saying that I'm a fucking soft ass nigga, but I'm not about to be out here trying to hurt you. I know every man uses that line, but that's not me. Just as much as you have some fucked up shit happen to you, trust me I've had some fucked up shit happen to me.”

Alexis looked to see Quinton eyes glossy.

“My own step mother has driven a wedge in between me and my father. My father was in love with my mother and quite honestly I think he still is but he's lying to himself. My pops wasn't always a preacher. He used to be heavy in the drug game. To this day, even though people know him as Bishop, it ain’t cause of the church. Back in the day he was known as Bishop because of the fact that he was the ruler of the streets. When he met my mom, she was working in one of the trap houses. They started fuckin around and they had this whole ghetto hood love shit. But him and his wife, my step mama, they were together from day one. Back in the day, supposedly my step mom was that ride or die chick. Like hard. She was down for that nigga no matter what. Then he started fucking around on her with my mom, and my mom got pregnant. When she had me he didn’t want me and told her that he didn't want nothing to do with me. And she was actually cool with keeping it that way for a while.” He scoffed.

Alexis felt sorry for him. “You don’t know that though Quinton.” She whispered.

He gave her a knowing look. “Trust me. I know. He acted like she just didn’t exist anymore. But one day she had enough, and she showed up at his house. My Pops told me that my step mom attacked her while he was still holding me, after he told my mom that he was wrong and that he would take care of me. He promised my mom he wouldn't let nothing happen to her. But shit didn't work out like that. Step moms crazy ass went and shot herself and shit, mad at my pops trying to kill herself. After that, my dad decided he didn't want to be in the drug game no more. He promised himself and God supposedly that if she lived, he would get out the game. Well clearly she lived so he kept his promise. They ended up getting married and my sister was born a few years later. Me and Niecy tight as hell, but sometimes I'm wondering how she could come from such an evil person.” He growled.

“What you mean?” Alexis asked.

“My Pops didn't like the fact that I hung out with people that were still in the drug game. I mean I understand it at and all, but I'm not him. I got my own life too. So me and him don't necessarily see eye to eye. And she don’t help because she always got something smart to say and he don’t say shit. I think he's the reason why my mom is the way she is.” He said.

“What’s wrong with your mom?” Alexis inquired.

"After my Pops stopped hustling, he told my mom that he couldn't fuck with her like that no more, and she started drinking. You gotta understand my pops has been the only man my mom has ever loved. One of them Romeo and Juliet type shit. Like she couldn't even think about herself with another dude. She used to drink mad heavy too. I mean she's cleaned up now and everything, she's got her own practice and stuff, but keeping it real, she still love my father. Keep it real, I mean I think they still fuckin around, I just can't prove it. I really don't care if they do. But the shit that pisses me off is that he can be a hypocrite." He mumbled.

"But how can you make him to be a hypocrite just because he still messes around with your mother? I mean if anything, wouldn't that be something that you would want?" Alexis asked confused.

"Nah man. Him staying in the pulpit and preaching about forgiveness and about being one big happy family and all that shit, when he got more skeletons in his closet than the damn cemetery itself with all the hoes he done fucked." Quinton barked.

Alexis listen to what he was saying and was utterly surprised. *Yeah I'm definitely not going to tell this nigga that I fucked his daddy.* She told herself.

"I couldn't imagine not speaking to my father." She voiced. "He's all I have."

"Well," Quinton said. "Just like your pops is all you have, my moms is all I got."

Alexis shook her head. "So do y'all even talk?" She asked.

"Somewhat." He answered. "I still go to service every now and then so I can check on Niecey, but as far as everything else goes, I think he's just pretty much written me off. Besides, he's too busy trying to keep his wife happy because she's threatening to leave him every second of the day. Last I heard, she kicked him out because he cheated on her with some young chic and one of the members saw them, I don't know."

Oh shit! She thought. *Oh God this can't be happening! How could someone have seen us? We were in his office!* She tried to turn her attention back to his conversation.

"But, all I can do right now is worry about myself. And now, well I guess I got to worry about my seed." He said looking at Alexis.

Alexis squirmed uncomfortable. "I mean Quinton I appreciate that and all but you're forgetting one key factor." She mentioned.

"What's that?" He asked.

"You have a girlfriend. I've said this so many times, like I don't know how many more times I can say it. You have a girlfriend! And after everything I just told you, I really don't need any more drama. How do I know that your girl ain't the type to just run up on me and try to kill me? Hell how do I know that she ain't the type of chick that won't fuckin hire a damn private investigator?" She spat.

Quinton thought about what she said. "I mean I can't really say that you wrong. Will she be pissed off? Hell yeah. But that's some shit I gotta deal with." He promised.

"But that's what I'm saying Quinton. It won't be just you that's got to deal with that shit! It's going to be me too. Because whether you want it to or not, this shit's going to trickle down to me. Honestly, how do you expect her to react when she finds out you got another girl pregnant?" She asked.

"You right." He agreed. "But right now, that's all I can do is deal with the consequences. I mean I know shorty is jealous and yea she gonna pop off. Yeah she going to be mad. But, I mean let's keep it real, I know she out there doing her thing too. Other shit that I gotta deal with shit, at the end of the day, she knew the type of life that I was living." He assured her.

"Wait hold up." Alexis stopped him getting angry. "So you expect me to trust and believe that she wants to be with you even though she is out here doing her own thing, but you sitting here telling me to my face that she's just going to understand the type of lifestyle you lead? I don't understand how you expect me to take you serious when you say stuff like that Quinton! Like how is that reassuring me that you going to be there for me when you basically about to dump the next broad to get with me? I can't believe anything you say!" She yelled. "Like that's fucking trifling as hell!" She said.

Quinton sighed frustrated and dropped his head in his hands. “I'm not saying that I'm trying to wife you or nothing like that. But damn it Alexis, you are carrying my baby! Shit, at this point, we're gonna have to deal with each other for the rest of our lives! We got a fucking baby on the way. Hell no I wasn't expecting to bring a kid in the world right now, but the baby is coming and it ain't shit I can do about it. So the only way that I can spin this in my favor, is if I just let her know that shit is what it is. Let me handle her. I already know she'll be fucking pissed off. I can handle that! I already know she going to do everything possible to try to get at me. But at the end of the day, we ain't got no papers. At the end of the day, we ain't married. At the end of the day, I'm a grown ass man and I'm gonna do what the fuck I want to do. And this grown ass man is going to take care of his responsibilities! Point blank. I'm not one of these other niggas so don't come at me like that!” He told her.

Alexis chose not to speak and remained quiet. Quinton looked over and saw the fear in her eyes.

“Look shorty,” he said. “I didn't mean it like that. I wasn't trying to scare you or nothing. But come on. I need you to stop stressing over the small stuff. We just gotta handle one thing at a time. Right now, you said you got a problem, I'm going to try to help you fix it. And while you fix that problem, I'm gonna eliminate another one. I don't know what's going to happen in the future as far as between me and you, I know you're saying you don't want to be in a relationship right now, and I can respect that. We don't really know much about each other. But what I do know, I'm feeling.” He smiled at her.

Alexis gave him a small smile and felt herself blushing.

"You bad as hell. You smart, you not trying to just be living in the projects or relying on somebody else to take care of you for the rest of your life. That's the type of chick I want in my corner. Can I take care you? Yeah. But I want to be with a chick that knows that she can handle her own. Tierra used to be like that. But she's comfortable with the life that she's in. She's comfortable being my girl and being out in the street. I don't want to be with a chick like that. I want to make sure that my shorty wants for nothing, but, be able to get it on her own if need be. Because if something happens to me, I don't want to know or think about my shorty slumming it because she don't know how to fend for herself." He explained.

Alexis looked at him and nodded her head in understanding.

"I guess. I didn't look at it like that. But, I just needed you to understand where I'm coming from." She told him.

"I do." He said. "Trust me I do. I just don't really let that show because the way I get down, you can't really show weakness. You can't really show love like that. Love will get you killed." He said.

"Oh trust me I know." Alexis agreed.

She looked at the clock on his car and saw that it was almost 9 o'clock.

"Damn we been out here a good minute." She said noticing how dark it had gotten.

Quinton looked around and noticed as well. "Damn you right. Alright so what's the game plan with this chic? What you trying to do?" He asked.

Alexis told him about her lunch date with Ariane and began to put her plan into action.

*

Chapter Seven

"Hey girl!" Ariane greeted Alexis opening her door.

"Hey girl how you doing?" Alexis greeted giving her the fake church hug.

Alexis smiled at Ariane seething on the inside. Ariane stepped back to let her into the house. Alexis, not trusting her, rushed her.

"Girl get your stuff let's go! My stomach is growling!" she insisted.

Ariane noticed her urgency. "What? You can't come in for a few minutes?" She asked.

Alexis laughed nervously. "No it's nothing like that. I'm just hungry and haven't eaten all day. I was trying to wait to eat because I know if I would have eaten earlier, I wouldn't have eaten anything. I've been waiting on this old food all day! This restaurant is the bomb.com!" she told her.

"Ok." Ariane said. "Give me a second, let me grab my stuff."

Arian walked out of Alexis eyesight to gather her things. Alexis stepped into the foyer of the house and looked around. Alexis wondered where her brother was.

"This is a nice house." Alexis said out loud.

She could hear Ariane moving around in the back.

"Thanks girl." She heard from the distance.

"So where's your brother?" Alexis asked.

"Oh he had to work." She responded. "He'll probably be back the by the time we're done." She told her.

"Oh okay." Alexis tiptoed to the mantle that held pictures. She picked one of the photos up to see Ariane and JayShawn smiling.

“Yeah something's not right with this bitch.” she said to herself.

She hurried to put the photo back when she heard Ariane coming back into the living room. She ran back over to the door so she would not get suspicious. Ariane came through the living room with her bag.

“Girl my bad. I had to fix my lips chile. You ready to go?” She asked.

Alexis laughed again. “Yeah I'm ready. Girl we just going to get something to eat. We not going to the club.” She joked with her.

“Girl this is Atlanta!” she replied. “I always go to make sure I'm dressed to impress. Shoot you never know I could meet my baby daddy while I'm out.” She laughed.

Alexis shook her head and followed her out the door. “Trust me girl, Atlanta nigga’s ain't all they're cracked up to be.” She told her.

“Hmmm if you say so.” Ariane said. “I'm trying to meet me a tall, dark and handsome kind of man.” She continued joking.

Alexis smiled a little wondering if she should leave. “I can't with you.”

She walked to her car and unlocked it for Ariane to get in. She turned to see her walking towards her car.

“You don't want to ride with me?” She asked.

“Nah I was just going to take my car so that way when we finished eating, I could go ahead and finish running errands and stuff.” Ariane told her.

“You sure?” Alexis asked. “I don't mind driving.”

“No its okay.” She assured her. “Besides, this way when I'm ready to go, I can just go.”

“I hear you.” Alexis said. Inside she was upset. She needed to get Ariane alone where there was no way for her to escape.

“Unless you want to ride with me.” She heard her offer.

“Girl bye.” She exclaimed. “I'm the exact same way as you. If I go somewhere, I want to be able to take my own car. And that's anywhere I go.” She said so she wouldn’t sound offensive.

“I don't blame you.” Ariane responded. “Well I'm following you.” She said as Alexis climbed into her car.

“Alright cool.” She responded.

Alexis cranked her car and pulled out of the driveway. She drove to the restaurant while Ariane followed behind her. Alexis sent Quinton a text message with the change of plans.

Alexis: We just left. Stay tight. She drove her own car. She's following behind me.

Quinton responded a few moments later.

Q: I got you.

Alexis got closer to the restaurant thinking of how she was going to get Ariane to confess that she killed Collin. The more that she thought about it, the coincidence was too great. She gripped her steering wheel while driving. *If this bitch had anything to do with Collin being killed, she's going to regret the day she met me*. She promised herself. Moments later she pulled up to the restaurant and the two of them parked their cars. Alexis sat in her car for a second and contemplated backing out. The thought of Collin losing his life and everything that she had been through flashed before her and she quickly changed her mind.

"I can't be afraid." She said to herself looking in the rear-view mirror. "I got to go through with this. This has to end otherwise I'm going to be running for the rest of my life."

Ariane was close to the car so Alexis got out. The two of them walked towards the door of the restaurant.

"Damn girl I can smell the food outside!" Ariane pointed out.

"Yeah the food is good." Alexis agreed. "What's that saying, food so good, make you wanna slap your mama?" She joked.

Ariane laughed. "Long as I can get me some ribs and some macaroni and cheese," she told her, "I'm good."

"Well you bout to be doing great after you eat this food." Alexis told her.

The two walked inside and were seated at a table in the back.

"So how long you been in Atlanta?" Alexis asked.

"A couple of weeks. Just trying to get adjusted and everything. This is such a big town compared to Greensboro." She admitted.

"Greensboro was the town of Mayberry." Alexis laughed. "Everything is bigger than Greensboro."

The two girls shared a laugh and the waitress brought back their drink orders.

"So what are your plans since you're in Atlanta now?" Alexis inquired.

"Well I was thinking about getting back into school, but right now I mainly just trying to find a job. I don't want to be living with my brother for too long." She informed her.

"Ok. Sounds like a plan. So what's been going on in Greensboro?" Alexis asked. "Have you heard anything else about the case?"

"No not much." Ariane said looking down at her phone.

Alexis could tell she was a little nervous, but she didn't push.

"I did have to go and talk to a detective one time about the shooting that happened at the trial and my recollection of it, but aside from that, I haven't really spoken with anybody. I just want to put it behind me right now." She answered sadly.

"I'm sorry." Alexis said dryly.

"No need to apologize." Ariane told her. "You did nothing wrong." She answered with a sigh. "It was JayShawn that was messed up in the head. I can't believe that I dealt with him for so long. What was I thinking?"

Alexis not sure what to say remained quiet. The waitress came with their food and it gave the two women something to focus on.

"You wasn't lying!" Ariane exclaimed. "This food does look good."

"Yep!" Alexis agreed. "A friend of mine brought me here a couple of months ago and I've been hooked ever since." She laughed.

"A friend?" Ariane's interest piqued. "Is he cute?" She asked.

Alexis laughed. "It's nothing like that trust me. He was just there for me during a tough time when my grandmother died."

"Oh I'm sorry to hear that." Ariane apologized. "I didn't know your grandmother passed away."

Yes you did bitch. Alexis thought.

"You ok?" she heard her ask.

"Huh?" Alexis asked. "Yeah I'm fine. It's still a little hard to deal with. My grandmother was my everything. But knowing that she doesn't have to deal with cancer anymore makes me deal with it better. I was angry for a while. But I know that I have an opportunity to make her proud and that's what I'm going to do."

Ariane shook her head. "I'm sorry to hear about your grandmother. Losing somebody is never easy. Especially when it's somebody you really love." She said looking off.

Alexis couldn't take it any longer. "You know what? You're absolutely right. We both had a lot of losses. You lost JayShawn. And I'm sorry. I really am sorry. You loved him. But you know what? I gotta be totally honest with you, I hate him. The shit that he did was unspeakable. I'm not going to apologize for the way that I feel about him. He was a monster. You may love him, but you clearly knew a different side of him." She said eating her food. "Although, it wasn't too different because if it was, you never would have called the cops on him that day. I was there when he hit you. You just didn't know it. That was nothing compared to what the fuck he did to me. The shit that he did, only the devil could do something like that. Him and that crazy bitch."

Ariane rolled her eyes. "I don't even want to talk about that hoe."

"Well," Alexis continued. "You may not want to talk about it. But I do. Because it's some stuff that you clearly don't know and need to understand. Your boyfriend raped me repeatedly and damn near killed me. I'm not saying it's your fault but I don't see how you can sit there and cry and get all depressed over somebody that can do some stuff like that. I've lost a lot of people that were close to me because of your boyfriend. I lost my best friend, my boyfriend, hell he killed his own sister!" she said her voice escalating. "What kind of person can do something like that? So excuse me if I'm not send up here boo-hooing because of some fuck ass nigga that deserves to rot in hell. I'm not trying to take it out on you, but this nigga did some really fucked up shit."

Ariane was fuming on the inside, but she had to continue to play her part. She didn't want Alexis to know how angry she was with her, so she pretended to be hurt.

"Don't you think I know that? I know he did some really messed up stuff okay?" she hissed. "I knew he had issues but if I knew that he was capable of that, don't you think I would have done something?" She cried.

Alexis had no sympathy in her heart. "I don't know." She told her with an attitude. "The last time I saw you, before all of this went down, you were popping off at the mouth because you thought I was after your boyfriend. But now that you see what he's done, all of a sudden you want to be my friend? Why? Why did you call me to warn me about Collin? Why all of a sudden did you come here and pop up out the blue and want to see me? From my standpoint, it seems a little shady. Not to mention, that I saw you at the cemetery the day of my grandmother's funeral."

"I-I-I uh." Ariane said.

"You what? There's no point in denying that you were there. One of my friends told me that he saw you. So what? You stalking me or something?" Alexis snapped.

"No!" she snapped. Ariane had to think fast. "The only reason I was there at the cemetery is because I wanted to apologize to you for everything that had been done. I know it's not going to change anything nor is it going to bring anybody back, but I felt like I could at least apologize. I could at least do that. That's it."

"So then why didn't you approach me then?" Alexis asked. "Why sit there and take off?"

"I don't know." Ariane lied. "I guess I didn't really think it through. Plus it was your grandmother's funeral and it just wasn't the right time. I got ready to come over there but I just, I couldn't do it. I didn't know how you would react." She told her.

"Hmph." Alexis grunted. Even though Ariane's explanation seemed feasible, Alexis just couldn't let go of the alarms going off in her head.

"Okay so what is it that you want exactly?" Alexis asked her.

"I wanted you to know my side." Ariane stressed.

Alexis took a bite of her food to give herself time to calm down. Ariane picked up her glass of water and took a long sip before she began.

"Look," she started. "When I first met Jay Shawn, everything was cool. I helped him out with a couple of things, and he was really sweet."

Alexis held up her hand to stop her. "Personally I really don't want to hear shit about yals relationship, because that has nothing to do with me. No offense, but all I'm concerned about knowing is what the hell happened with my friend." She said.

Ariane nodded her head in understanding. "Sorry. Basically around the time that you came into the picture, JayShawn was just cold hearted. He was messing with this girl chic and me at the same time. The day that I came over there and he got arrested, he sent me a text telling me that he missed me. He said that his girl was doing some shady shit and he wasn't tryna get caught up in that and that he wanted us to go away. He didn't tell me what exactly was going on, he just said that he needed to get away for a while. I told him I would think about it. I was all set for it until I came to the house and saw him with that girl. I just don't understand why he kept playing me like that." She explained.

Alexis fidgeted in her seat. Ariane saw her frustration.

"Yeah I know you don't want to hear about that part. Anyway, all I remember was a bunch of arguing and he hit me. I mean he had kind of pushed me around before but nothing that extreme. And I got mad and I called the cops. I wasn't going to but I couldn't lie about the bruises. When he got arrested, I thought he was going to get out in a couple of days or something. But then I found out about everything else that happened, I really didn't know what to say. He started writing me when he was in prison, and he told me that he didn't do any of that stuff. He said that you came to him and that you were trying to set him up because y'all didn't work out. That's why I didn't like you." She told her.

Ariane was impressed with how good she could lie and make it sound believable.

"I didn't know that he actually did all that stuff to you Alexis." She promised.

“So you didn't know anything?” Alexis asked. “How could you not know? This dude had a record about as long as my damn arm. Hell the first time I met you, I told you to your face that I didn't want your dude. But you did what typical females do. Instead of coming at him, you came at me. I had a man. Somebody that I cared about and loved, but your man took that from me. So fuck no I'm not going to sit there and want to be sympathetic for you. Because the way I see it, you're part of the problem.” Alexis spat.

Ariane wanted to reach across the table and slap her, but she kept her cool.

“Look, when I found out that JayShawn got out, yes I should have told you. But, I didn't think he would come out to you.” She expressed.

“How could you not?” Alexis asked. “This idiot was in prison because of me. So you didn't think that when he broke out he wouldn't try to go to the person that got him locked up in the first place? Any muthafucka would do that! He held a grudge! That’s common sense.” She fussed.

Ariane held her head down. “Alexis, I can't take any of it back. I'm not the one that did it. That's why I called you. When I found out what JayShawn did to Collin, I called you. Because I knew you would want answers. If that was me, I'd want answers.”

“So then you know about the other killer?” Alexis asked bluntly catching Ariane off guard.

“Huh?” Ariane asked looking startled.

Damn I didn't know she knew about that! She thought. “Wait, what are you talking about?” She asked feigning ignorance.

“The detective that handled the case called me and told me that JayShawn didn't kill Collin. So I'm right back where I started.” Alexis huffed.

"Well, I honestly don't know anything about it." Ariane pleaded. "I thought it was JayShawn. I mean he just seemed so spiteful and when he escaped, it was right around the time that it happened."

"Uh huh." Alexis said.

The waitress came back to check on them.

"Can we get the check please?" Alexis asked her.

"Not a problem." The waitress responded. "Did you want to separate the check or did you want it together?"

"Separate." both Ariane and Alexis answered.

"Ok." The waitress told them. "I'll be right back."

"Look," Ariane said after a few moments of awkward silence. "Clearly this might have been a bad idea. Maybe we can try to talk at another time."

"Yeah." Alexis agreed. "Maybe." She said.

Or maybe you won't. She thought.

The waitress brought the check and the two girls payed for their meals.

"I do appreciate you asking me to lunch." Ariane said. "I'm still trying to learn the area, and despite what you think of me, I hope we can at least be cool." She told her.

Alexis shook her head and got up to walk towards the door. She walked to her car with Ariane following.

"For what it's worth Alexis, I'm sorry." She apologized. "I really am." She said.

"It's straight." Alexis told her. "We'll talk soon." She promised.

She got in her car and started the ignition.

"All right." Ariane shrugged off.

She turned to walk to her car. Getting in and closing the door, she let out a frustrated annoyed sound.

"I hate that bitch!" She growled.

She started her car and began to drive.

"Well finally we know the truth."

Ariane jumped when she heard the voice behind her. She looked in her rear view mirror to see Quinton sitting in her backseat with a gun pointed at her.

"What the fuck are you doing in my car?" She asked. "Who are you?"

"Don't worry." He told her. "It won't matter soon. Drive."

*

Ariane woke up to see herself in an empty room with little furniture tied to a chair. She immediately began to struggle to get free.

"What the fuck are you doing?" She screamed. "Let me go!"

Getting no response she yelled again. "Let me go!"

Quinton smirked. "Not just yet. We got business." He said.

"Why are you doing this? I didn't do anything." She told him. "Please." she pleaded. "Please let me go."

Ariane could hear the clicking of high heels coming down the hall. Seconds later Alexis appeared standing by Quinton.

"Oh… she's finally awake?" She taunted.

Quinton moved out of the way so that Alexis could get closer.

"You sure you want to do this?" He asked her.

Alexis looked at him and gave him a look that made him nervous. She turned her attention to Ariane.

"So this is how this is going to work." she said. "I'm going to ask you some questions, and you're going to answer them. If you lie to me, you suffer. Plain and simple. Got it?" She asked.

"What the hell?" Ariane cried. "Alexis I don't know what the fuck is up with you but I didn't do anything! You need to let me go cause you're fucking tripping!"

"Oh no I'm quite clear in what I'm doing." Alexis told her. "You see cause I've been doing a little bit of investigating on you, and I've learned some things. Like how you were with Collin the day that he died. Yea, didn't think I knew about that did you?"

Ariane remained quiet.

"Yea so while you thought you was stalking me, I was stalking your ass right back. So, you're either going to tell me what I need to know or…."

"Or what?" Ariane asked trying to sound strong.

Alexis walked up and stood close to Ariane.

"Or my face will be the last thing you see." She stated with confirmation.

Ariane wrestled with the handcuffs that bound her trying to break free.

"This is bullshit!" She yelled. "Your ass is fucking crazy!"

"I might be." Alexis agreed. "But, I will get my answers. See the thing is, I know more about you than you think I know Ariane. I know that you said that you're living with your brother, but, I had some people look into it. Your brother doesn't live with you. In fact, your brother lives in Buckhead with his wonderful fiancé. He rents the house you are living in to college kids. You should be more careful in hiding all of the evidence. A quick search through your house and I found out everything I needed to know." She informed her.

"You were in my muthafucking house? Are you insane?" She asked.

Alexis laughed. “Funny, I was about to ask you the same thing.” She said. “I know that you've been following me for the last couple of months. I know that the day that Collin went missing you were seen with him on campus. I know that JayShawn didn't kill him. I know for a fact that you have no family here aside from your brother. So I know that you weren't coming to the cemetery to apologize. So now, would be the time for you to tell the truth. Because if you don't, I would hate to think that your brother would spend the rest of his life finding your body parts.”

Ariane looked at Alexis with hate and spat in her face. Quinton jumped up to grab Alexis but she held up her hand. She walked over to the table and picked up an instrument walking back to Ariane. She held her head up to see Alexis grab her finger with a pair of pliers. Alexis squeezed hard cutting her fingertip off. Ariane screamed out in agony.

“I don’t have time for these games.” Alexis barked. “Like I said continue to lie and play stupid, then you'll suffer. So it's better that you be honest now. Otherwise,” she wandered off turning her back to Ariane.

Ariane sat tearful and kept her head down.

“Fuck you!” She grumbled.

Alexis smirked and took the gun that was sitting on the small table. Quinton had made sure to put the silence her arm so that even if someone was in earshot of the isolated house, they would not hear. She turned to look at Quinton.

“Wow.” She said. “For somebody who damn near about to die, she sure has guts.” She placed the gun on Ariane’s right leg and pulled the trigger.

“Arrrggghhh!” Ariane cried out in pain. “Fine.” She said through gritted teeth as she tried to control her breathing. “Fine. You wanna know, I'll tell you.”

Alexis sat in the chair opposite her leaning forward to listen.

"I fucking hate you." Ariane said. "I hated you the minute that I fucking met you. You was walking around acting like you was the shit and you wasn't. JayShawn was fucking acting like you was just that bitch and I couldn't understand why. It's all your fault!" She growled. "If it wasn't for you, me and him would be together right now. If he wasn't so busy chasing after you, he would be with me. He wouldn't have had to go to jail. My baby wouldn't have died!"

Quinton head turned towards Alexis. Alexis looked genuinely surprised.

"What baby?" She asked.

"I lost my baby. Me and JayShawn was going to have a baby and he was excited about it. He wanted to be a daddy. I wrote him letters while he was in prison telling him about how we were going to be a family. He promised me that when he got out we would be together. But all he ever talked about was you. So I wanted to get rid of you once and for all. When I saw Collin, I took my opportunity. I thought that he would lead me to you but he didn't. So, I killed him." She hissed.

Ariane felt her blood boiling as she listened to everything that Ariane said.

"I listened to him gripe and moan and complain and beg for hours. And that shit got old and fast. I couldn't take it anymore. So yes, I killed him. And I don't regret a damn thing I did. You took everything from me. You have no idea what I've been through. I couldn't have my baby daddy with me when I lost my baby because he was too busy on you. I wanted you dead. If I wasn't tied to this fuckin chair I'd kill your muthafuckin ass too bitch." She said with malice.

Alexis felt the room spinning she was so heated.

"So you killed Collin because your man, your so call baby daddy attacked me? You've got to be fucking kidding me. Collin didn't do shit!" Alexis said tearful.

Ariane smiled seeing her cry. "You took my man, so I figured I'd take yours." She said.

"You bitch!" Alexis lunged at her fury taking over. She hit her over and over with the gun until Ariane lost consciousness. She must have blacked out because she felt Quinton pulling her off of him.

"Lex, stop!" he yelled. "Just stop."

Alexis lunged at her still body again but Quinton grabbed her and held her back.

"No!" he said. "She's gone. It's over." He told her.

Alexis dropped the gun and broke down in tears shaking.

"She killed Collin. She killed Collin." She repeated over and over. "I can't do this anymore." She wept.

Quinton grabbed Alexis holding her tight as she fell in his arms.

"Why?" She cried. "Why did she do this? He didn't deserve that."

"I'm sorry Lex." Quinton whispered kissing the top of her head holding her tight. "I'm so sorry."

Alexis pushed away from Quinton and grabbed the gun that he took from her. She turned towards Ariane and walked over to her.

"What are you doing?" Quinton asked.

Alexis pointed the gun over Ariane and pulled the trigger putting a bullet into her body.

"Now it's done." She whispered.

*

Six Months Later…

Chapter Eight

"Alright Alexis you know the drill." The nurse said. "Now this is going to feel a little cold."

Alexis lay on the table with her bra on while the nurse put the gel on her stomach for her ultrasound.

"Alright let's see how the little guy is doing." The nurse started.

She began the ultrasound and almost immediately Alexis heard his heartbeat. She could see him moving on the screen and her heart melted.

"This little guy is active today huh?" her nurse joked.

Alexis smiled looking at her son.

"Yeah he is. Just like his daddy."

Alexis turned to see Quinton responding to the nurse and grinning proudly. An uneasy feeling came over her as she waited for the nurse to finish.

"Alright so it looks like you're about to get into your 36th week. Are you having any discomfort or pain?" She asked.

"Not really." Alexis told her. "Just some pressure every now and then but nothing that I can't handle." She said.

"Okay. Well now's the time where you're going to have to really start taking it easy. No stress." She urged. "You got about a month left before he makes his debut into the world. Have you decided on a name yet?" She asked smiling.

"Oh this is a junior right here." Quinton spoke up.

The nurse smiled. "Of course." She said. "Alright I'm going to go ahead and step out so you can get cleaned up and dressed."

The nurse stepped outside and Quinton walked over to Alexis to help her sit up.

"You good?" He asked looking at her noticing her grimacing when she sat up.

"I'm fine Q. It's just a little bit of pressure." She said.

Quinton smiled softly. "Alright."

"Quinton you know you don't have to come to these appointments with me." Alexis told him. "They're just check-ups."

"I know." He said. "But as long as you are carrying my son, I'm not going to miss anything. That's what is important right now." He told her pointing to her belly.

He placed his hand on her stomach and felt the baby move.

"Ay yo this boy is hype right now." He laughed.

Alexis smiled a little. "Don't I know it? And when I lay down it don't get no better." Alexis said.

She felt uncomfortable again and shifted in her seat. "Okay I need to go ahead and get cleaned up." She said changing the subject.

"Alright cool." He agreed. He went to the chair and grabbed her shirt.

Helping her put it on he smiled as he looked at her closely.

"Boy your belly getting big." He teased.

Alexis rolled her eyes annoyed. "Whatever. Everything on me is getting big. I can't wait to get this boy out of me." She huffed. "Can you take me to get something to eat since you insist on being up under me?" She asked him.

"Of course. And what you want?" he asked.

"Oooo I have been craving chicken all day." She told him. "Popeye's." She blurted out excited.

"Popeye's?" He asks disgusted. "That stuff is too spicy. Spicy food is not good for you right now." He told her.

"Um excuse you but if I recall, I already have a daddy." She said laughing.

"Ok." He said caving in.

She hurried to finish getting dressed and the two walked out of the office to the car. Alexis pulled her cell phone out of her purse to see that she had missed messages. Her father had text messaged her to check on her to see how she was doing. She thought that he would be upset when he found out that she was pregnant, but he had been really accepting. Although she could tell that he was disappointed, after a couple of weeks he started to come around. He had even going to a few appointments with her when Quinton couldn't.

Quinton made sure to introduce himself to her father despite Alexis wishes and promised her father that he would be there. And he hadn't disappointed Alexis yet. She couldn't make a move without Quinton being there. She texted her father to let him know that the appointment went well.

Alexis: Everything is fine with the baby. He's really active. ☺ Going to get something to eat.

Daddy: Okay baby girl. Glad everything went ok. Call me when you get home.

She looked at the missed call and saw a number that she didn't recognize. She hit the call back button so that she could identify who it was. After a few rings a male voice picked up.

"Hello?" the voice answered.

"Yeah this is Alexis. I had a missed call from this number?" She asked as Quinton helped her get into the car.

"Alexis this is Bishop. I think we need to talk." He told her.

Her attitude changed and she became stiff.

"Okay." She said "I can't really do that right now because I'm out and about." She told him hoping that he would take the hint. "But you can make an appointment if you like." She suggested.

"Can you stop by tomorrow?" He asked her.

"Tomorrow is a little tight as far as my schedule." She disputed. "However I do have an opening today after 5 o'clock." She said.

"Ok." He said. "Where would you like to meet?"

"How about the original spot?" She rushed.

He knew that she was referring to the church so he agreed.

"Okay that's fine. I will see you then." He said.

"Ok." She answered. "Talk to you then." She hung up the phone.

"Everything okay?" she heard Quinton asked.

"Yeah everything is fine. It was just my boss telling me that she wanted me to come in for an evaluation. It's coming up on the end of my internship so I have to do a bunch of surveys and whatnot." She lied.

"Ok cool. When is it?"

"Later on today." She told him. "She's just going to come to my house to make it easier."

"Yea that makes sense." He said. "Alright we'll go ahead and get you something to eat and get you home so you can rest a little bit." He told her.

Just as Alexis had hoped, they ended up going to Popeye's and Alexis stuffed herself with her favorite chicken. Quinton laughed as he saw her greasy face smiling with happiness.

"Dang if I knew that all I would have to do is get you some chicken to get a smile out of you, I would have bought the damn restaurant a long time ago." He joked.

Alexis flipped her middle finger up at him. "Look, I'm carrying around an extra 30 pounds with this baby. It's hot, my feet are swollen, and I can't see my cooch anymore." She fussed. "So if this makes me happy, then let me eat my damn chicken. You better quit messing with me before I come across the table."

"Gotta catch me first." Quinton said teasing her.

She threw a balled up napkin at him and he blocked it laughing.

"Ok ok I surrender. I give up before you start throwing chicken bones." he said.

His phone vibrated on the table and he picked it up. Looking at the screen he frowned and dropped it back on the table.

"Man I ain't got time for this shit." He said.

"What's the matter?" Alexis asked frowning.

"Just Tierra." He answered. "She being petty right now. She done started messaging me again."

"Well Quinton what do you expect? It's a lot for her." She explained.

Alexis felt guilty knowing that Quinton broke up with her and her not even knowing if the baby was truly his.

"You don't think that she would rat you out or anything do you?" Alexis asked concerned.

Quinton scoffed. "Hell no. She's not stupid. Besides, her hands are dirty too. Even if she did do something like that, she knows it's too many people that would get her. I'm not worried. And you shouldn't be either. Tierra is all mouth." He assured her.

"I mean still." Alexis said. "If we hadn't have done what we did, yal would still be together now."

"Yeah we may have been together for a short amount of time, but, I still know that it wouldn't have worked between me and her. She's got stuff that she does that I don't agree with, and I don't rock with it like that. You just relax shorty. At the end of the day, my most important concern right now is in your belly. And I ain't letting nobody stop that." He wiped the corner of his mouth.

"You shouldn't be worried about some random chic that don't matter to me." He told her.

"I guess." She answered. "I just know how it feels."

"See shorty that's the type of stuff that I'm talking about." He told her.

"What?" She asked confused in between bites.

"That's why I'm feeling you. You don't even know her like that but you are concerned about her." He pointed out.

"Well it's not necessarily being concerned about her," Alexis said "It's more so being concerned that you don't get locked up because she's spiteful. Or that she doesn't come after me in any way. Females nowadays are ruthless. I mean I hate that I have to keep bringing it up, but look at my situation. That bitch killed my boyfriend because she was mad that her man was coming after me. I mean yeah I may have done a little harmless flirting, but I wasn't out like throwing myself at him."

"Well that situation is over and I don't want to hear you talking about it again." Quinton said sternly.

Alexis looked at him and saw his facial expression. "What's the matter with you?" She asked with an attitude.

Quinton looked around and looked her in the eyes. "I saw a different side of you that day." He said. "I understand why you acted that way, but I'm not trying to get you caught up in stuff like that." He told her.

"I know that you don't." Alexis snapped. "But I'm a big girl. And besides, that needed to be handled by me. I needed answers. And I got my answers and I handled it so what are you tripping on?" She asked.

"I'm not." He said wiping his hand with the napkins. "I'm just saying I really don't want you doing no shit like that again." He told her. "If you have an issue that needs to be handled, just let me know."

"Well shit I don't plan on having any other issues like that." She told him wide eyed. "Right now I just want to eat and go home and take a nap before evaluation." She stressed.

"Alright cool." He agreed dropping it. "Come on penguin." He teased.

He started calling her penguin on account of how she waddled when she walked.

"Fuck you Q." She grumbled.

"Aw such cute terms of endearment." He laughed kissing her on her cheek.

She shoved him away and he helped her to the car. Alexis got into the passenger seat and relax falling asleep before they even got out of the driveway.

*

Bishop led Alexis into his office offering her his chair.

"Thanks for meeting me." He told her.

“Uh huh.” She answered dryly. “Are we alone this time or what?” She asked. “Cause I heard that last time I was here that one of your members was here and saw us or whatever.”

“No. It's just me. I made sure of that.” He said.

Alexis looked skeptical.

“I locked the doors to the church, so nobody can get in unless they have a key.” He explained.

“That's comforting.” She said.

“Look,” he started. “I just needed to talk to you to see what exactly is going on.”

Alexis looked at him and smirked. “You got to be kidding me. You wanted to see what was going on?”

She looked down at her stomach “Well clearly I'm not carrying a basketball around Bishop. Yes I'm pregnant, and yes there's a possibility that it's yours.”

“A possibility?” He asked his eyebrow shooting up.

“Yes Negro I didn't stutter!” She responded with an attitude.

“So then what I’m hearing is true?” He questioned.

Alexis sat back and folded her arms across her chest upset. “And what exactly are you hearing Bishop?” She asked.

Bishop cleared his throat before speaking. “Well, a few of the church members said that you and my son were seen together quite frequently.”

“Ok and?” She hissed. “I mean damn Bishop just go ahead and ask the question you really wanna ask.” She demanded.

“Ok.” He said. “Is there a chance that the baby could be his?”

"Well I guess we'll know the day that he comes out. Because unfortunately I made the mistake of sleeping with two men in the same damn day and now I'm carrying a child and don't know for sure whose it is." She griped.

Bishop sighed. "How could this happen?" He groaned.

"Well gee I don't know Bishop. It happened because we had sex? It happened because we had unprotected sex. I didn't do this by myself." She snapped annoyed at his attitude.

"I'm not saying that you did Alexis. But you gotta understand my situation. I have a wife, and a family." He explained.

She scoffed. "Well according to Quinton, you don't have much family left." She hinted.

He looked up sharply at Alexis. "So you and Quinton have been discussing me?"

"Don't get cocky. Nothing like that. You're not that important. Now look," she said. "I'm not going to sit here and act like I'm innocent or something because I know I'm not. And believe it or not I'm sorry. I didn't mean to come into your life and destroy it in any manner. I really don't want or need anything from you. You have a family and I understand that. But, I wasn't the only one that did anything that day. I didn't have sex with myself. It does take two Bishop." She pointed out.

Bishop rubbed his temples in frustration. "I realize that. I'm not saying I'm 100% innocent either. I should have stopped you and I could have stopped you. But I didn't. It was just something about you that I couldn't resist at the time. Even now looking at you, something just takes over."

Alexis felt a little squeamish and uncomfortable hearing him say that. "Well right now the only thing is taking over me is this baby." She claimed.

The two sat in an uncomfortable silence for a few moments. Bishop looked at Alexis sitting in his chair with her round belly. He motioned his hand out towards her stomach.

"Is it okay if I touch?" he asked.

"Yeah go ahead." She agreed.

He placed his hand on her stomach and felt the baby moving.

"Wow." He admired. "Do you know the sex yet?" He asked.

She smiled a little. "Of course I know the sex. I'm due in a month." She said. "But it's a boy."

Bishop nodded his head taking it in. "A boy huh?" He said. "Well, I don't know that it's going to be easy, but I'm not just going to completely bail on my child, I mean if it proves to be mine." He told her. "I'm pretty sure that it's going to cause more trouble than I would want for the both of us, but I made the mistake of not being around when Quinton was first born, and I'm not doing that again." He promised.

Alexis shook her head in agreement. “Yeah Q told me about that. I don't want to complicate things Bishop. I've already started to prepare myself to take care of the baby on my own. I don't want to drag Quinton through this. Hell he's already broken up with his girlfriend for me. I know he said that he was going to be done with her anyway, but he wouldn't have even had that option if I hadn’t put myself into the situation. So it's better that I just kind of back away. My life is turning into a real life episode of Maury Povich right now, and the closer that I get to this baby being born, the more scared that I get.” She explained. I mean all I can think about is what happens when the baby comes out? You and Quinton look so much alike. And I don't want to be one of those women that has the baby and intentionally has a man that is taking care of this child his entire life and I know that there's a possibility that it's not his. I don't want to be that type of parent.” Alexis felt herself near tears so she rushed to leave. “Look I gotta go ahead and get home. I'm supposed to be relaxing and having a stress free pregnancy. So much for that.” She said. “Like I said, don't worry about it. I'm not going to say anything. And I'm pretty much going to tell Quinton the same thing. After I have the baby, I'm planning on just leaving. That’s just the best resolution for everybody. Quinton can go on with his life, your wife and family doesn't have to find out and it won't affect you in the church.” She said.

She struggled to get up out of the chair and Bishop helped her.

“That's all right. I got it.” She broke away. “I gotta start getting used to doing stuff by myself.” She said.

She walked over to the door opening it and her heart began to beat rapidly as she stared in Quinton’s eyes.

“Q!” She whispered. “What are you doing here?”

Quinton looked as if he could spit fire. "Funny thing is I actually came up here to take your advice and talk to my father." He said pissed off. "So when were you going to tell me?"

"Tell you what?" She asked nervous.

He stepped inside. "Come on now. Don't play stupid. I heard everything. When were you going to tell me that you fucked my pops?" He asked. "I mean what? Were you even planning on telling me that this might not be my baby?"

"Son," his dad called out.

"Oh, you still trying to call me that? Or were you talking to the one she's carrying?" He said spiteful.

"I deserve that." His dad replied.

"That's about all that you deserve. Cause for real, you don't deserve half of what you got with your selfish ass. And you," he said turning his attention to Alexis. "You and my dad? Are you serious right now? But you not a hoe though. Yea right."

Alexis felt tears stinging her eyes at Quinton's harsh words.

"Quinton I promise you, I didn't know. It was a mistake. It happened the day that my grandmother died. I was upset, and I came here to ask your dad to do the eulogy for the ceremony. I don't know why I did it. But I did. I can't take it back, and I'm sorry. When it happened, it was just a whole bunch of emotions. And you gotta believe me, I felt so guilty afterwards. Before I know it I got caught up." She explained.

"So you mean to tell me when I saw you in the parking lot at the church, you told me everything that else that happened, but you couldn't tell me about you fuckin my pop?"

Alexis held her head down and remained quiet.

"Son." Bishop started. "Don't be upset with her. I could have stopped it and I didn't."

"Of course not." Quinton scoffed. "Why would I expect you to act like a human being? Hell why would I expect you to act like a father? You never have before." He pointed out.

"Okay that's enough." Bishop said. "Regardless I'm still your father."

"Barely." He said. "I'm out. Fuck both yal."

Quinton walked out the door slamming it behind him. Alexis sat down in the chair rocking back and forth trying to get herself together.

"I'm so sorry." She cried to herself. She stood up to leave and felt a sharp pain. "Ouch!" She cried out.

Bishop turned to see Alexis bent over in pain.

"Are you okay?" He asked.

"I think I'm in labor." She grunted.

A few seconds later she let out another scream. Bishop rushed to his table to pick up the cell phone and call 9-1-1.

"Yes this is Bishop White at Mount Zion. I have a young lady here in my office who is pregnant and believing to be in labor." He instructed.

He gave the emergency operator his address and hung up the phone.

"Okay just relax. They're going to be here in a second. Do you have anybody you can call?" He asked.

Alexis slowed her breathing. "I'm fine. It was just the pain was a little too much. I can call my dad and have him meet me at the hospital." She said. She pulled out her cell phone and called her father. "Hey daddy. Can you meet me at the hospital? I think I might be in labor. I'm not sure."

Alexis paused for a few moments listening to her father's panic. "Well right now I'm at the church. Waiting on the ambulance. Like I said I feel okay for the most part, but I just wanna go to the hospital to be sure."

She could tell her dad was panicking on the other line and looking at Bishop so was he. He looked as if he had aged several years over the course of a few minutes.

"Just meet me at the hospital okay?" She said calm and breathing slowly.

A few moments later the ambulance arrived. Bishop looked frazzled as if this was all new to him. She looked at him frustrated.

"Just don't worry about it." She said. "When I know more I'll let you know." She said.

The EMT assisted her wondering what the two were talking about.

"Are you her father?" he asked

Alexis scoffed. "More like the father." She mumbled.

His eyebrows shot up after hearing what she said and quickly assessed what they had just walked in on. It was at that point that Alexis realized that she was about to go through it alone and she felt the familiar knot in her throat as the EMT's rushed her to the hospital.

*

"Okay Alexis." Her nurse told her. "It does look like you're showing the early stages of labor."

"But I'm only nine months." Alexis claimed.

"Oh it's normal." The nurse reassured her. "In some cases first time moms go into labor as early as seven months. You know I've even had one woman go in as early as six months and the baby made it. No worries. Your little boy will be just fine." She said not realizing she was making Alexis worry more. "Normally we would send you home until you were farther dilated, however the doctor felt it would be better to keep you for observation because he noticed a few problems with your chart." She said.

"What problems?" Alexis inquired worried.

"Well for one, your stress test was a little high. At this point in your pregnancy you really should be more careful as to the amount of stress that you're dealing with. So just as a precaution, we're going to go ahead and keep you." she told her.

"Believe me I'm trying." Alexis responded.

"It's okay." the nurse reassured her again. "Just try to relax as much as you can because too much stress can hurt the baby. She said.

The thought of her son being hurt worried her more. She tried to block everything out of her mind so that her son would be ok.

"On a scale of 1 to 10," she heard the nurse question, "What is your level of discomfort?"

"I would say about a six right now." She answered. No sooner had she said than Alexis felt another contraction. "Make that a ten." She moaned trying to breathe. She cried out several curse words as she dealt with the excruciating pain.

"Yep I remember this game all too well." the nurse joke. "Just breathe through it honey. It'll help." She instructed her.

Alexis tried to listen to the nurse but the pain was becoming too much. The kind nurse came over and squeezed Alexis' hand.

"It's okay. You're doing well. Do you have anybody that I can call for you?" She asked her.

"Yeah my father should be here by now." Alexis realized.

"Okay. I can try to locate him for you." She offered. "What about the child's father?" she pushed.

Alexis shot her a fierce look. "I don't want him here." She spat.

"Okay." The nurse conceded. "I understand. I didn't mean to upset you hun. I'm going to go and call your father for you. Just try to relax as much as possible okay?" She told her. "And remember to try to breathe through it." The nurse stepped out of the room and Alexis lay back to breathe.

She closed her eyes so that she could attempt to relax. The nurse's advice worked because she found herself feeling peaceful and calm despite the craziness she had experienced that day. But it was short lived as a few minutes later she heard a knock at the door and was interrupted.

"Come in." she called out assuming it was her father, her eyes still closed.

The door opened and a short white man wearing an all-black suit stood at the door. She could see his gun and shield from the door.

"Can I help you?" She asked.

"Alexis Thomas? "He said.

"Yes." she answered nervous.

"My name is Detective Genesis. I'm with the Atlanta Police Department." He introduced himself.

"Okay?" She asked annoyed. *Damn can I have this baby in peace!* She thought.

"I realize this might not be the best time to talk with you, however I have an important matter to discuss." He apologized.

Alexis sighed. "So much for stress free." she mumbled. "Well, right now it's kind of a little bad timing. As you can see I am about to spew life from my body at any given moment." She spoke sarcastic.

The detective shook his head with no expression. "I understand. But this matter is urgent. Have you spoken with the detective in Greensboro regarding the case of Collin Strong?" He questioned as he sat down in the chair across the room.

"Yeah but it's been a minute." Alexis answered.

"I'm sure you been made aware of the update on the case right?" He asked.

"Yeah. Last time I talked to the detective he said that he believed that there was another killer besides JayShawn." She said feigning worry.

"Well," the detective started, "We believe that we have tracked the killer. A woman named Ariane Suites." He said.

"Who?" She asked playing ignorant.

"Ariane Suites." He repeated. "She was the ex-girlfriend of the deceased JayShawn Cheston."

Alexis pretended to think for a few moments. "Oh yea I think I remember seeing her at the trial before the shooting." She wandered off.

"Yes. She was in attendance. Witnesses say that they saw her with Collin the day that he died. It was hard to trace her because at the time of his death apparently she was pregnant." He told her.

"Oh God!" She cried out loud placing worry in her voice. "Well can you guys find her? Do you have her in custody? Am I safe?" She rambled off concerning questions.

"Actually, we tracked her here to Atlanta and she disappeared off the grid. It wasn't until a few weeks ago that we confirmed her as a suspect. As our luck would have it, apparently someone got to her before we did." He informed her.

Her face showed genuine surprise at what she was hearing from the detective.

"What do you mean?" Alexis asked still playing ignorant.

If she could give herself the Academy Award for the performance of her life, she would.

"Well her body was found in some run down house near Buckhead." He told her. "She was shot a few times, and lost a lot of blood."

He talking like this bitch is alive. She thought to herself. "Oh dear God." She whined. "That's so horrible. I hate to hear that. Did they find out who killed her?" She pried for more information.

"She's not dead." He told her. "She almost died but the doctors were able to save her. If it wasn't for some teenagers horsing around and breaking into the house, she wouldn't have been found until it was too late. She will have some long term damage because of her injuries sustained, but, we have her in custody. We are awaiting trial where she will be extradited back to Greensboro." He explained.

Fuck! You've got to be fucking kidding me. I just knew I killed that bitch. She thought.

The detective looked at her face noticing her reaction. "Are you okay?" He asked.

"Yeah it's just a contraction." She quickly responded faking her breathing to cover her lie.

"I'm sorry. I know you are going through something right now." He said "Let me go get your nurse for you."

"No wait." Alexis called out. He turned to look at her. "Do they have an idea of what's going to happen? From what it sounds like she got enemies seeing as how she got people just running around here trying to kill her."

The detective nodded his head. "In this world, we all have enemies. But unfortunately we can't find out anything right now because her jaw is still wired shut. She took a pretty bad beating."

Alexis smiled on the inside remembering how she attacked her. But on the outside she was fuming. She changed her demeanor quickly so that the detective wouldn't catch on.

"Well please just let me know whatever you need. I can't really do anything right now obviously, but, I want to help in any way I can." She offered.

At that point a real contraction hit and she screamed out in pain. The detective took that as his invitation to leave and quickly left the room leaving Alexis to her pain.

"Fuck!" She screamed.

The nurse popped her head in. "Hey sweetie. I got your dad out here with me. You want him to come in?" She asked her.

Shit. Alexis thought. She really hoped that her father did not see the detective leaving her room. She couldn't stand to deal with a barrage of questions at the moment.

"Yeah that's fine." She said sitting up.

Her father came into the room worry all over his face. "Hey baby cakes." He said. "How you feeling?"

“Really Daddy?” She asked sarcastically. “I feel like I have to poop out a Buick.” She retorted.

Her father laughed at her. “Didn’t nobody tell your ass to get pregnant.” He joked.

Alexis rolled her eyes. “Whatever.” She said. “I'm okay for the most part. Just dealing with these contractions. It is the worst pain I've ever felt in my life.”

“Until the baby comes out.” He pointed out. “Then that's going to be the worst pain.” He happily reminded her.

“Thank you for pointing that out Daddy.” She said dryly.

“You’re welcome!” He said grinning at her giving her sarcasm right back. “Now where is that knucklehead ass boy of yours? He should be here to witness his child being born.” He snapped. Even though he accepted Quinton as the father, he still didn’t like him.

“Relax daddy. It's still early. I don't want him to worry about anything until they were for sure that I was in labor.” She said.

Lying there, she felt the sudden urge to use the bathroom and before she could get up, her legs were dripping wet. “What the hell?” She said in a panic.

Her father and looked at her in panic. “Well now is the time for him to worry.”

Alexis got nervous realizing that her water broke. Her father rushed letting her know he was going to get her doctor. As soon as he left the room she struggled in scramble to her phone. She texted Quinton as fast as she could.

Alexis: I'm here at the hospital. In labor. Water broke. We also have another major issue. That bitch ain’t dead.

She hoped that Quinton would respond to her message. She didn't want her father ready to kill him for something that was her fault. She put her phone down and her doctor and a string of nurses walked into the room.

"Well from what I'm hearing your water broke Miss lady?" The doctor asked cheerful.

Alexis was starting to get irritated with everyone's happy attitude.

"Well why the hell else would I be here?" she hissed.

"Watch your mouth." Her father told her.

The doctor just laughed. "Trust me I've heard a whole lot worse. And I have a feeling that in a few hours I'm going to be hearing a whole lot worse from her." He shrugged it off. "In this profession, we get cussed out on a daily. As a matter of a fact, it's pretty much almost every hour. It's a part of the territory."

"Still." Her father said giving her a disapproving look.

The doctor put his gloves on and sat down at the edge of the bed. "Okay Alexis I need you to lay back so that I can check and see how dilated you are." He instructed her.

Alexis complied with his request and relaxed. The contractions were becoming more severe and increasing so she knew she wasn't going home anytime soon.

"Looking good. Coming along quite nicely. About six centimeters right now." He told her.

"Really?" she asked. "I wasn't as dilated a few hours ago." She thought out loud.

"Well, it looks like he's ready to make his entrance." One of the nurses spoke up. "You could potentially have a quick labor and delivery at the rate you're going."

"I hope so." Alexis grunted feeling another contraction.

Her father stood near the door not able to handle seeing his daughter in pain. It was to his relief that Quinton came through the door so that he could leave. Alexis looked up to see his face and felt happiness for a brief moment.

"And here's the proud father." The doctor exclaimed. "Come on in and get comfortable. Gonna be here a bit."

Quinton came in and walked to the other side of the bed near Alexis.

"Okay well, we are going to come back in a few hours and check on you. In the meantime, enjoy your last few moments of not being parents." He joked.

"I'm going to go get something to eat from the cafeteria." Her father told her.

She could see how uncomfortable he was so she tried to put his mind at ease.

"Daddy its ok. Quinton's here now so why don't you just go ahead and go home? It's not like I'm about to have the baby right now." She smiled.

"No I'm fine baby girl. Besides, this is my first grandchild about to be born. I'm not going anywhere." He told her. "But I am going to go get me a bite. Can I get you anything? Ribs, greens, chicken?" he joked.

Alexis laughed at her father's humor and lay back. "Go eat grandpa."

He left the room and Alexis was alone with Quinton. Quinton sat down in the chair not speaking.

“So I'm assuming that you’re still mad with me?” She asked. “Look Quinton you have every right to be upset. Believe me it was not intentional but what's done is done. Right now, I'm really worried about this baby and this whole Ariane thing. I’m scared about what could happen to both of us. She's not dead.” She stressed. “She's alive. She hasn't been able to tell anyone so far because her jaw is wired shut. But what happens when it's not? I don't want to go to jail. And I know you don't either.” She said.

“It'll be handled.” Quinton told her not really looking at her.

“How?” She asked. “This girl is surrounded by police in their custody. How in the hell is it going to be handled? Eventually she's going to go to trial and she's going to tell them that we tried to kill her. Well I tried to kill her. I keep messing up.” She rambled ready to cry. “Sorry. I'm so sorry.”

Quinton remained quiet and let her get it out. “Like I said don't worry about it. I have it taken care of.” He was upset but he masked his feelings for the time being. “Right now you just need to worry about little man.” He told her.

Alexis shook her head in understanding. “Quinton for what it's worth, I really want you to know how sorry I am. I really hope that you are the father.” She stressed. “I know that me and your dad messed around once, but I don't want to destroy his life. I don't want to destroy yours either. I sometimes wonder if I should even be in existence.” She said.

Quinton cleared his throat and stood up to leave the room. “I gotta make a quick phone call. I'll be back in a few minutes.” He got up and walked up.

Alexis was left alone in the room where she let her emotions take over.

Chapter Nine

Alexis heard a tap at the door and saw Tiffany walk in. She had seen her a few times in the hospital from work and when she initially found out that she was pregnant.

"Hey girlie!" Tiffany said.

"Hey." Alexis greeted her dry. "I guess you're working maternity tonight?"

Tiffany smiled at her. "Yup. For the next twelve hours. How you feeling?"

Alexis bit her lip and spoke softly. "I need to have the baby tested when he's born."

The nurse's mouth dropped open and formed a perfect O. "Um…O….Ok." She stuttered.

"There are two men that could potentially be the father. One of them just left, and the other one well he's from the same family, it's a long story." She told her. "But I need to have the baby tested and I need the two men tested and I absolutely need this to stay between us." She said. "And I mean it." She reiterated.

"Okay." The nurse agreed. "I'll take care of it. I'll go ahead and get the DNA on Quinton, and you just let me know when I need to take the DNA of the other one." The nurse informed her. "When the baby is born and we take him back for initial tests, I will add that one to the list. I will just need your consent form. Don't worry it'll be handled." She promised.

"Thank you. Um, do you think that I could get a pen and some paper?" Alexis asked.

“Sure.” Tiffany told her. “Just give me a minute and I'll be right back.” She told her. “When Quinton comes back in the room just tell him to come to the nurse’s station.” She instructed.

“Thank you.” Alexis said feeling grateful.

“No problem sweetie.” She smiled. “And believe me, it's going to be okay.” She said to help her relax. “I'll be right back.”

Alexis lay down and thought about everything that had transpired over the course of the last couple of years. She wondered on her existence and why she had not just died that day. The nurse interrupted her thoughts bringing her the pen and paper that she requested.

“Here you go hun.”

“Thank you.” Alexis told her.

“No problem sweetie.” Tiffany said walking towards the door. “You buzz me if you need me.”

Alexis sat up in the bed and pulled the tray closer to her and began to write.

I sit here and wonder if life is really meant for everybody. There are so many wrongs in my life that I don't know how to make right and I've hurt a lot of people. I'm taking my frustrations and fear out on others and I'm not dealing with any type of pain properly. Because of my behavior, some people have died, people have killed, and more people have been hurt than I can count. I broke up families. It's not something that I'm proud of either. So many times I have contemplated just taking myself out of the equation, that way I know no more lives have to be ruined. I know that I can't take it back and I honestly feel like even if I had the ability to, some things I know I wouldn't. As I write it, I realize how messed up it sounds with everything that I have done. Looking back on it, I wish I had died that night at Jayshawn's apartment. Because if I had, Collin, Summer, Tameka, they would all be alive right now. I wouldn't have destroyed a marriage and caused a man to die, and even though he deserved a brutal punishment, because of my actions, JayShawn is dead also. I have people's blood on my hands and as much as I want to ignore it, the guilt is killing me. I now have a beautiful baby boy that was brought into this world in unfairness. Because of my stupidity, one of the first things that I will remember of his life, is trying to figure out who his father is. I hope that my son knows how much I love him no matter the mistakes that I've made. And whatever God decides in His plans for me, I accept it wholeheartedly. I can't keep running from my wrong doings. I can't hide any longer. I no longer can think about myself because now I have to think about my son. I want my son to know that his mother is a strong individual that wants nothing more in life than for him to be happy. I want my son to know that even though his mother has made a lot of bad choices, that he is nothing but a child of God. To those that I've hurt, I'm sorry.

To those that I have wronged, I apologize. God forgive me for the ultimate sin that I have committed.

Alexis folded the piece of paper and slipped it in her purse that lay at the foot of the bed. Shortly after Quinton came back into the room.

"Hey." Alexis said. "I know now may not be a good time, but I want to go ahead and make sure as far as the paternity. The nurse said you can come by the station and she'll do a DNA swab. That way we can determine who the father is because I don't want to make another man pay for something that's not his. If you want to walk away, I understand. I know that it will be difficult and I want my son to have his father in his life, but the way that I went about it was wrong. So if you want to walk away, I won't fight."

Quinton looked at her for a few moments before he spoke. "You can keep the apologies. I already went to the nurse's station. She had already told me. I asked her when I came in to do a DNA test. So that's already handled. And since you wanna keep harping on it, I'm not mad. You did what you did. Don't get it twisted, it's really fucked up that you did that with my pops of all muthafuckas, but at the end of the day, it's over and done with. I don't want to be thinking about that when this child comes into the world."

"But Quinton how can you not?" She asked. "It's all I've been thinking about since I got here. This whole ordeal is fucking with me. The baby coming early, this bitch Ariane won't fucking die." She whispered so that no one would hear.

"Alright hold up." He stopped her. "I already told you I got that other situation handled. Now if you really want me to be cool about all this, just focus on having the baby right now." He advised.

"Okay." She agreed softly.

Alexis looked at Quinton and his cold hearted demeanor. She knew that he would never forgive her for sleeping with his father, but she didn't want to exasperate him with the issue. He sat down in the chair and turned the television on. Alexis lay back on her pillow and closed her eyes saying a prayer in hopes that God would hear her. She jumped up to the most severe pain that she had ever felt.

"Q go get the doctor!" She yelled.

Quinton jumped up and ran over to the bed. "What's the matter?" He asked.

"Go get the doctor! I feel like I need to push!" She grunted trying to control her breathing.

He hit the button on the remote to call for the nurse. He yanked the door open to get the nurses attention. Several nurses came running in and Quinton panicked.

"Look she says she thinks she needs to push." He told them.

"Okay well don't worry hun, its ok. That just means she's getting out of the labor and ready for delivery. It's expected. She's been here for several hours and has progressed quite nicely." the head nurse informed him. She looked at Tiffany and instructed her to go and get the doctor. "Okay Alexis let me check you really quick. Try to relax. I know it hurts right now but I really need you to not push and try to relax." She instructed.

"Okay." Alexis whimpered.

Seconds later her father and doctor ran in and Alexis let out a loud scream.

"I can't take this!" She yelled.

Her dad ran over to hold her hand as did Quinton.

"Come on baby you gotta listen to the doctor." Her dad told her.

"Okay Alexis looks like you're ten centimeters. Right on time. Okay, we just need to get you prepped and then you can start pushing okay?" The doctor assured her.

"Oh hurry up!" she moaned.

The doctor kept on her words not affecting him. "Okay dad and grandpa, I need you to help pick her up and help her hold her knees."

Her father looked as if he was ready to pass out. One nurse noticed it and offered to take him out side.

"Mr. Thomas why don't we step outside while she gets prepped?" She suggested. "You look like you might need to take a seat."

He looked at his daughter who was in pain and felt helpless.

"Go Daddy I'll be fine." She said squeezing Quinton's hand harder and one of the nurses took her father's spot.

She sat in an upright position with her knees to her chest and bore down so that she could finally push.

"Okay Alexis." the doctor began. "On the count of three I want you to push as hard as you can okay?" He said.

"Okay." She grunted.

"1…2…3."

She squeezed Quinton's hand and pushed as hard as she could.

"Shit!" She cried out.

"Alright good, good, you're doing good. Give me one more." The doctor instructed. "Count of three. One, two, three."

She pushed again feeling as if her body was ready to rip open. "Oh God this hurts!" She screamed.

Quinton kissed her hand and rubbed her head. "I know, but you're doing good shorty." He told her trying to encourage her. "Come on ma little man is almost here."

"The fuck you mean come on? You not the one pushing his ass out of your fucking body! Why don't you push him out of your fucking dick?!" She snapped.

He looked around to see if anyone had a reaction or heard what she said. The doctor looked at him and gave a quick smile.

"It's okay. She's just speaking out of anger right now from the pain. She won't even remember saying that in a couple of hours." He told him.

Alexis cried out again as she felt more pain. "Please get this kid out of me!" She yelled.

"Alright, let's get you back in position." The nurse told her. "Ok are we ready to push?"

"The fuck you think?" Alexis snapped.

"Yep she's a feisty one." The nurse joked. "Okay Alexis time to push. Come on push." She encouraged.

Alexis pushed as hard as she could and the doctor stopped her.

"Alexis. We have a problem. I need you to stop pushing." The doctor commanded.

"What's the matter?" Alexis asked. "Why can't I push?"

The doctor spoke quickly and quietly. "It looks like the umbilical cord might be wrapping around his neck. So I need you to stop pushing so that I can try to pull him out okay?"

Panic wore all over Alexis face and she looked at Quinton. Masking his feelings he tried to stay strong for Alexis.

"It's going to be ok." He told her. He grabbed her hand and held it tightly. "It's going to be okay right?" He asked stern as if he was challenging them to say something different.

“It will be.” the nurse said. “Just don't push.”

“Ok Alexis, I'm about to go in there and see if I can get the cord removed okay?” the doctor advised.

Alexis nodded her head in understanding unable to speak.

“Nurse I'm going to need some clamps.” The doctor rushed.

The nurses quickly moved to assist the doctor so that he could help deliver the baby safely. Alexis lay trying to see what was happening and feeling the discomfort for what seemed like forever until she heard her son's first cry. She smiled and tears of joy took over.

“Oh my god.” She exclaimed. “He's beautiful!” she cried looking at him.

“He is.” Quinton agreed tears threatening to fall from his eyes.

“Well mom and dad say hello to your beautiful son.” The doctor said smiling.

The head nurse walked over handing Alexis the baby. She looked down at her son and smiled.

“Well hey handsome.” She sniffed. “I'm your mommy. You are so handsome.” She told him.

The baby lay in her arms eyes barely open appearing to be squinting at her.

“He's gorgeous.” She murmured.

He wrapped his tiny hand around her finger. Alexis was in shock.

“You know I'm your mommy huh?” She said.

Looking down at him she admired until she felt a sharp pain.

“Oh God!” She gripped her son to make sure that she didn't drop him.

“What's the matter?” Quinton asked confused.

"Shit I'm still in pain!"

The doctor looked at the screen monitoring her and the baby in awe.

"Oh dear." He said. "This is rare."

"What?" She asked in agony.

"Nurse," the doctor instructed. "I need you to grab the baby from Alexis. Alexis, I need you to bear down again and push." He ordered.

"Ok, why?" She asked.

"There's another baby."

"What?" She and Quinton both asked at the same time.

"Yes". The doctor confirmed. "It appears to be another baby. I need you to push one more time for me as hard as you can." He told her.

Alexis looked at Quinton fearful.

"It's okay babe. I'm right here." He promised. "Now bare down and push." He told her.

Alexis gritted her teeth and pushed as hard as her body would allow. A few minutes later the doctor pulled out another baby.

"Oh no." He whispered. He held his head down and handed the baby to the nurse.

"Let me see." She requested.

"I'm sorry Alexis." The doctor said solemnly. "She didn't make it."

"She?" Quinton questioned.

"Yes. It looks like you had a daughter as well. I'm sorry." He apologized.

Alexis allowed the tears to fall.

"How could she not make it? Was it something that I did?" she cried. "How could she be there and nobody see her?"

"It happens." The doctor told her. "It's rare but it happens. In the ultrasound, she could have been a shadow, and we would have just thought that it was your son."

Quinton held his head down.

"Can I at least hold her?" Alexis asked.

The doctor looked hesitant but he allowed it. Alexis kissed her forehead and Quinton looked down at his daughter.

"I'm sorry baby girl." He whispered, a tear falling from his eye.

The nurse came and took the baby while Quinton embraced Alexis so that she could cry.

"It's okay." He said. "It wasn't meant for us to have her. It just wasn't our time. We still have a beautiful son to take care of." He comforted her.

"I'm going to go ahead and get your son cleaned up." Tiffany told her taking the baby out of the room. The doctor and nurse finished cleaning Alexis up and wheeled her to the recovery room.

*

Alexis woke up to see Quinton sitting in the chair in the corner of the room holding the baby. She smiled at the image and spoke softly so as not to frighten them.

"Hey." She whispered.

He looked up and gave her a smile. "Lex, he is smart. He's been gripping my hand since I picked him up. He got quite a grip." He joked. "Just like his daddy."

Pain stabbed Alexis in the heart hearing him say that.

"Quinton, maybe you shouldn't get too attached until you know the results. I mean, I still gotta call your dad and let him know. He doesn't even know I had the baby." She said.

"It's already handled." He told her looking back down at the baby. "He came earlier and was swabbed. The nurse said we should know within a couple of hours." He told her. "I know he's mine." He said matter of a fact.

"Even still." Alexis reasoned. "I just don't want you to get attached and then the doctors come back and say something that you don't want to hear, and you flip out or something."She said. I don't want that to happen. I want the baby to be yours trust me."

"He is. Quinton White Jr." He stated.

"You didn't sign the birth certificate did you?" She asked worried.

"No. The nurse said she was going to wait for you to wake up before she came around to get the parents information." He told her. "But I thought we agreed we're going to name him Jr?"

"Yeah I mean we did. But that was before…you know." She trailed off.

He cleared his throat and stopped her.

"Like I said. He's going to be named after his father; me."

Alexis not wanting to argue, let it go and held out her hands motioning for him to bring the baby. He stood up and handed him to her carefully.

"Hey man." She smiled.

The baby had been cleaned up and she kissed his soft head.

"You scared us a little bit coming early." She said. "But I'm glad that you're here. Mommy definitely has to do better so that her son doesn't have to worry about anything." She said. "I promise you, you'll never have to worry about anything pumpkin, mommy always got you."

A soft not came at the door and Alexis looked up to see her father.

"Hey grandpa." she greeted him grinning.

"Wow." He said choked up. "My little girl is a mom now." He proclaimed. "He's beautiful. What's his name?" He asked.

"Junior." Quinton answered before Alexis had opportunity to say anything.

Her father looked between the two and shook his head chuckling.

"I see. Well, I am happy for the both of you." He said. "Now let me hold my grandson." He demanded.

Alexis smiled and held her son up for her father.

"He's a big one." He joked.

"Don't I know it." Alexis laughed.

The three sat and admired the beautiful creation that had just been born. Alexis fell asleep to her father cooing over the baby. A few hours later she woke up and Tiffany was coming in to check her vitals.

"Hey there mommy." She whispered. "How you feeling?"

"Exhausted." Alexis told her.

"Well, it comes with the territory." Tiffany laughed.

"Oh you've got kids?" Alexis asked surprised.

"A daughter." She told her. "Listen, I don't have much time but um, I sent Quinton and your dad out for a few minutes and told them that I needed to check your stitches. But I have the results of the DNA test."

"Okay?" Alexis asked nervous.

"The test results came back 99.8% positive that Quinton is the father." She informed her.

Alexis let out a sigh of relief, not even realizing that she was holding her breath.

“Thank God.” She replied sounding relieved. “Can you bring the baby in here?” She asked.

“Sure. I'll be back in a few minutes because I really do have to check your vitals and stitches.” She said. “But I know that you need a few minutes.”

“Thank you Tiffany. I really appreciate it.” Alexis told her.

“Sure girl.”

She stepped outside of the office and Quinton came in. Alexis was beaming and he began to smile too.

“So we’re good?” He asked hopeful.

“Yes.” She laughed. “Yes you are.”

Quinton clapped his hands together in happiness. “I told you.” He said.

“Yep.” She smiled. “I can breathe a little easier now. Quinton White Jr. Watch out world.” She joked.

Looking at him, she became serious. “I know that me and you have a long way to go as far as whatever this is that we're doing, but, I appreciate you for being there. Not many men would have even wanted to speak to me after finding out what I did. I honestly expected you to walk away.” She said.

Quinton softened a little. “I mean don't get it twisted, the shit was foul, but at the end of the day, the results made me not even give a fuck about any of that anymore.”

Alexis listened intently.

“Our son ain’t gonna want for nothing.” He told her. “Whatever he needs you know I'ma take care of him and you.” He promised

“Well, I definitely plan on spoiling him too.” She giggled.

“Well we are definitely in for trouble.” Quinton joked.

For the first time that night, he laughed. Alexis felt so much better seeing him happy.

"You go ahead and get your rest." He told her. "Me and this little guy have to have a man to man talk."

"Oh Lord." She moaned dramatically. "Quinton the boy can barely open his eyes yet."

He laughed again. "He's my son. I know he understands everything I'm saying."

"Okay." She conceded laying back so that she could relax. She turned the TV on halfway paying attention to it. Closing her eyes, she rested.

Outside the door, Tiffany stood on her cell phone.

"It's done." She whispered. "I told her that Quinton was the father."

"Good." The person on the other end stated. "It should be $5,000 wired to your bank account first thing in the morning." they told her. "Nobody must ever know the real father's name." they reminded her.

"Absolutely." She answered hanging up the phone and walking back into the room to check on Alexis smiling at her secret and what was about to happen.

*

Prologue

"Okay mommy's little pumpkin, you ready to go home?" Alexis cooed looking down at her beautiful baby.

He lay in his car seat covered with a mesh blanket so that the cold winter air would not make him sick. Quintin smiled at Alexis with his son. It had been two months since their son was born, and even though he and Alexis still had their issues, they were starting to be a close family. He had fallen back slightly from the drug game for a bit to help Alexis out with the baby. And even when he was working, he was rushing to get home to him. He promised himself he would be the father to his son that Bishop wasn't to him.

"I'm going to go pull the car around." He told her.

"Okay." She responded not looking up from what she was doing.

Neither one of them happened to notice that there was a special news bulletin on the television screen. Alexis walked her son down to the car and the two headed home.

"Hey I'm going to go ahead and drop you guys off at the house. I gotta go handle a couple of things but I should only be gone for a few hours." He told her.

"Okay." She said.

She knew what he was going to go and do and even though she didn't like it, she was okay because she knew he would never put their son in danger.

"Why don't you just drop me off at my house then?" she requested.

She had been staying at his house for the last couple of weeks and was ready to return to her apartment.

"Now you know I like having yal at the house." He told her.

“I know.” She acknowledged. “But damn Q, you got me paying rent for a place that I'm barely at. I mean I'm only there maybe one day a week and that's just to get a couple of changes of clothes.” She said. “You gotta let me breathe just a little bit.” She joked.

“Alright.” He gave in. “But I'm coming over and staying here tonight.” He told her.

Alexis chuckled. “All right.” She said I guess that's better than nothing huh?”

“Woman long as you got my child, you going to always be close to me.” He teased her.

Alexis shook her head as they neared her apartment.

“Alright I'll be back in a couple hours.” He told her.

“All right.” She agreed. “I guess you want me to cook something huh?” She teased.

“That would be nice.” He laughed. He looked back at his side as she unfasten him from his car seat. “Tell her junior say, you gotta feed these men!” he joked.

Alexis laughed as she walked inside of her house. Quinton pulled off and she and the baby got comfortable in the living room. The baby began to fuss and she looked around for his formula.

“Shoot it’s at Quinton’s house. No worries munchkin, mommy can run right down the street and grab you some huh?” She whispered to him.

She put the baby back in the seat and rushed to the car so that she could get him some formula. Strapping him in, she hurried to the grocery store down the street. She came up on the railroad tracks and pressed her brakes to ease over the tracks lightly. Noticing her speed was not decreasing, she pushed the brakes a little harder.

“What the hell?” She said.

She began stomping on the brakes but nothing happened. Going down the hill her car picked up speed and Alexis panicked as she was approaching several vehicles.

"Shit!" She screamed she was now stomping the brakes swerving through traffic to avoid the oncoming cars, praying that her car would stopped. Quickly approaching an 18 wheeler, she swerved into her left lane not noticing the car that had just turned onto the street hitting her dead on. Her car flipped several times crashing over the small bridge barricade onto the ground below. Several cars stopped and pedestrians ran over to the see the car sitting upside down.

"Oh my goodness is she okay? Someone call 911!" Shouts rang out in the streets.

A few moments later, a small woman in a black sweat suit appeared next to the vehicle.

"It's okay!" she screamed. "I'm a nurse."

But what they couldn't see was her injecting Alexis with a very lethal dose of potassium chloride killing her instantly. She grabbed something out of the girl's purse and placed it in the front seat. Hearing the sirens, she grabbed the crying baby and disappeared quickly into the trees. She pulled her cell phone out, and made a phone call.

"Hey, it's Tiffany. It's done. The kid is alive though." She said rushing to her car that she had parked a block away.

She had followed Alexis from her house and got lucky that Quinton wasn't with her. She had cut the brakes to her car days before but wasn't able to push through with her plans until she had Alexis alone. She and the baby was as close as she was going to get.

"You sure she's dead?" The voice asked.

"Positive." She confirmed "I told you I got you. Her ass got my sister locked up for killing her husband and some other dude. It was easy too cause I found that letter in her purse that she wrote at the hospital and it almost sounds like suicide." She told her.

"Good. That bitch took everything for me. If it wasn't for her my ass wouldn't be here now." She hissed. "Now come get me I'm around the corner at the park. Go all the way to the back."

"Cool." She agreed hanging up the phone putting the baby in the backseat.

She drove a few blocks away pulling into a park off the main road and driving all the way to the back as told. She got out and took the baby out of the car the same time a woman got out of a dark colored sedan.

"Alright I gotta move fast because I need to get out of here before somebody realizes that was me." she said handing her the baby.

"No problem." the mysterious woman said.

The girl turned to her car not seeing the woman grab a gun out of her pocket. She turned around just in time to see her pull the trigger unable to scream before the woman put two bullets in her head. Her body fell to the ground and the woman looked around. She grabbed the girl's purse containing her passport, social security card, and all of her identification that she instructed her to bring.

"Goodbye Ariane Suites, hello Tiffany Paige." She smirked.

She looked down to the now sleeping baby in the seat on the ground. Picking him up from his seat, she walked off towards her car. The baby began to whimper as she disappeared into the darkness.

"It's okay baby. Mommy's here."

Thank Yous

Well you guys this is the end of the road for Alexis! I know yal are probably mad but, I'm sure eventually all will be forgiven. Lol. Wow I can't believe that I am finished with my first series! This is such an AMAZING feeling! Thank you to everyone that has been rocking with me since day one on this! The emails, tweets and messages for the finale were overwhelming and it is MUCH appreciated.

First and foremost I thank God for giving me the gift to do this. Many people question this profession but I love it and the joy that it brings to people.

My husband Michael, thank you so much for always being in my corner and supporting me no matter what. You push me to keep going when I want to quit and give me so much motivation. Thank you love for sharing your life with me.

My children, my boys, mommy loves you SO much! Yal are the best thing that happened to me and I do this for yal for real.

My father and big supporter. I know that you are proud and thank you for NOT reading my books. Lol. Otherwise, I would be washing my mouth out with soap. We have a special relationship that no one can break.

My siblings all over the globe, Kise, Brandi, Lloyd, Kiaren and Kimani, I love my fam all day. We don't talk everyday but know I love you guys no matter what. Brandi, sis keep fighting, you are strong and I admire you so much. Kick MS's butt!

Royalty Publishing House, Porscha, aka Queen P, thank you for believing in me with this series and giving me a place. It makes me feel so special to be recognized for my work. I will never forget what you all have done for me.

My brothers and sisters of the Blue & White, Zeta Phi Beta & Phi Beta Sigma, thank you all for your CONSTANT support. Your texts, calls, email blasts mean so much. Special shout out to my favorite big brother ever Joseph (Brother Joseph!), you've been my A1 since day 1 and I always got your back til we old and gray!

My sisters and brothers of the Brown & Gold Family, Iota Phi Theta and Iota Sweetheart Incorporated, you guys are awesome. Thank you Terrika, Hammie, Amanda Chambers, the Allen sisters, Gabby, love my poos.

My close friends, more like family, Danielle, Jesse, Tasha, Jackie, Shonda Wade, Briona Cole, Daryl Johnson, JDot, Brittany Wilson, Cynthia, Janell, Doug thank you!

My hags, Keisha and Steve, thank you for helping me out on MANY occasion!

And last but definitely not least, thank you the fans for continuing to support, coming out to the signings and meet and greets, and always giving me great storylines! Yal keep your eye on me cause you never know what I'm gonna do!

~Kitty Kisses!~

CPSIA information can be obtained
at www.ICGtesting.com
Printed in the USA
LVHW051631141218
600503LV00023B/337/P